CAPTURING

Slick Rock 9

Becca Van

MENAGE EVERLASTING

Siren Publishing, Inc.
www.SirenPublishing.com

A SIREN PUBLISHING BOOK
IMPRINT: Ménage Everlasting

CAPTURING KYLIE

ISBN: 978-1-62740-508-9

First Printing: October 2013

Cover design by Les Byerley

Printed in the U.S.A.

PUBLISHER
Siren Publishing, Inc.
www.SirenPublishing.com

CAPTURING KYLIE

Slick Rock 9

BECCA VAN

Chapter One

Kylie Mailing hugged her best friend, Evana Woodridge. Tears streamed down Eva's face, as she smiled and motioned for Kylie to come inside the house. "God, I've missed you, Kylie."

Kylie leaned in and gave Eva another hug, and her breath hitched with emotion. "I've missed you, too, Eva. You have no idea how lonely I've been without you."

"Well, you're here now and that's all that matters. Come on and let me show you to your room and then I'll give you a tour." Eva led Kylie down the hallway to the guest bedroom and opened the door to show her inside.

"Oh, this is really nice, Eva." Kylie looked at the gray-green carpet, which contrasted well with the cream-colored walls and the dark timber furniture. She spotted a framed picture on the wall of Eva surrounded by Quin, Gray, and Pierson, all of them grinning as if they couldn't be happier. "You have no idea how lucky you are. Those three hot, sexy men adore you. What I wouldn't give to have a man look at me the way they do you."

"We're the lucky ones," Quin Badon said as he entered the room and placed Kylie's luggage on the bed. As he turned back toward the door, he snagged his fiancée around the waist and kissed her long and deep. Kylie turned away from the loving display, her face heating at the passion and love she saw between Eva and Quin. An ache formed in her heart and she barely stopped herself from trying to rub the pain away. She opened the door on the left side of the room to discover an adjoining bathroom. At least she wouldn't have share a bathroom with Eva and her men. Although she was very happy her sister of the heart had found the loves of her life and was happier than she had ever seen her, Kylie wanted what she had, but didn't think she would ever attract one man, let alone more.

When she turned around to see that Quin had finally released Eva and was heading out of the room, she walked back over to the bed.

"All three of your men are studs, Eva. How the hell do you keep up with them?" Kylie asked and then cringed at her tactlessness. "Shit, sorry. Don't answer that."

"Kylie, don't you dare start changing on me now. I love you just the way you are."

Kylie sank down onto the bed with a tired sigh. "You're about the only one."

"Now, that's not true." Eva sat down next to Kylie. "My mom thinks the sun shines out of your ass, and Jack likes you just fine."

Kylie snorted out a laugh, because for some unfathomable reason Eva's mom treated her like she was an adopted daughter. Ever since Eva's mom had found out that Kylie had no living relatives, she had taken her under her wing. Even though it had been three years since Kylie's parents' deaths—her father from a heart attack, and her mother nine months later after wasting away from a broken heart—sometimes she still couldn't believe she was only twenty-three and already parentless. After her mom had been buried with her dad, Kylie had sold their family home and bought an apartment. She didn't want to live in a house with so many memories. She also missed Eva more than she let on and had been seriously thinking about moving to Slick Rock, Colorado, to be nearer to her friend.

"I love them all so much." Eva's voice brought her back to the present. "I don't need to keep up with them. Quin, Gray, and Pierson are all so different and I love each of them for who they are. Quin is so serious most of the time and can be a real hard-ass. Pierson is more laid back and is always quick with a joke. And Gray, well, Gray is a mix of his brothers, and even though his feelings run very deep, he is the mediator of the three. He's always stepping in and keeping the peace. They each offer me something I need and fulfill me in ways I never could have imagined."

"They're lucky to have you, Eva." Kylie gave Eva another hug and then opened her bags to start unpacking. "So are you scared about getting married?"

"No," Eva replied with a glowing smile. "I can't wait to officially be Mrs. Badon."

Eva stood and helped Kylie put away her clothes. "The dress fitting is tomorrow at ten o'clock. I can't wait until you see my wedding dress."

"Me either." Kylie zipped up the empty bag and slid it beneath the bed. "How many are coming to the wedding?"

"Around eighty, I think."

"Wow, that's a lot." Kylie sighed and hoped she would be able to cope with being around so many people. She often felt claustrophobic in crowds and hoped she didn't make a fool of herself by having a panic attack.

"Not really." Eva headed toward the door. "I'd better go see if my men need help with making dinner."

"Is there anything I can do?"

"No. I know how tiring traveling is, just rest for now. Come on out whenever you want."

"When are your mom and Jack arriving?"

"The day before the wedding." Eva was about to pull the door closed but paused. "I forgot to tell you that my fiancés' cousins are going to be here tomorrow. They are staying until after the wedding and from what I gather, they are also looking around for a ranch to buy. Quin has asked them to stay here for as long as they like, and the same goes for you. I don't want you going anywhere until we get back from the honeymoon. Will you promise to stay in Slick Rock for a while?"

"Funny you should mention that." Kylie broke eye contact with Eva, worried about how her news would be received. "I decided to move here and have already leased my apartment."

Eva squealed and rushed back to Kylie. She hugged her tight and Kylie blinked rapidly as tears pricked the back of her eyes. "Thank God." When Eva released her, and she saw tears of happiness in Eva's eyes, she had a hard time controlling her own emotions. "I had this speech all prepared and was going to harangue you until you agreed to stay. Now I don't have to. This is the best wedding present I will ever get."

"Eva, are you okay?" Gray stopped in the doorway and looked at his fiancée with concern. "Are you having another cramp? Are you in pain?"

Kylie could see the love and worry he had for Eva and felt a little envious, but she smiled toward Gray, hoping he couldn't see through her façade. But she was also happy that Eva had three loving men who accepted her and looked after her. Eva had been born with congenital hip dysplasia, and because of all the surgery she'd had as a child, she wore a brace and often suffered debilitating cramps.

"I'm fine. I just had some great news." Eva hooked her arm into Gray's. As she led him from the room, she looked back over her shoulder. "I'll see you in a bit."

Kylie nodded and watched her friend retreat as Gray closed the door behind them. She sank down onto the side of the bed and pushed her palms against her eyeballs, trying to relieve the dull ache behind them. As much as she loved Eva and wanted to please her, there was no way she could share a house with strange men while Eva wasn't there. The wedding was just less than a week away, but that at least gave her a few days to find somewhere else to live while she was in Slick Rock, and if she couldn't find anything to lease then she would rent a room at the motel. At least that way she wouldn't have to worry about having men underfoot.

After gathering some fresh clothes, Kylie showered and then dressed in her comfortable jeans and a T-shirt. Once done she headed toward the large modern kitchen. The scents of cooking food assailed her nostrils. It had been hours since she'd last eaten and her stomach growled. What she saw when she entered the kitchen surprised her. Eva was sitting at the counter, leisurely sipping a glass of wine, while Pierson set the table and Quin and Gray bustled around, putting the last touches on the meal.

"Kylie, you're looking refreshed." Pierson winked at her. "Would you like a glass of wine?"

"Please."

"I hope you like meatloaf," Gray said as he began to carry the food to the table.

"I love meatloaf." Kylie sniffed appreciatively before bringing the bowl of mashed potatoes from the counter to the table.

"Sit your ass down," Quin said in a low but firm voice.

"Woof," Kylie responded without thinking and then cringed inside as her natural sassiness and defense mechanism kicked in.

Quin stared at her for a moment and then tilted his head back and burst out laughing. "You'll do."

Kylie shrugged off his comment, though she couldn't help but wonder what he meant. She would do…for *what*? She had no clue, but at least he didn't seem to have taken offense to her response.

"You look tired, Kylie." Gray's eyes wandered over her face.

"Traveling is always wearing on a person," she answered nonchalantly. She wasn't about to tell Eva or her men that it had been more than two weeks since she'd slept through the night. They had a wedding to worry about. They didn't need her unloading her problems on them right now. There was no way she was going to spoil their time by spilling her guts. She'd never been one to lean on anyone.

They all talked as they ate and Quin explained that his cousins, Xavier, Lachlan, and William Badon were arriving sometime tomorrow from Dallas, Texas. "They finally had enough of answering to rich assholes with no manners and resigned from the security company where they worked as bodyguards. They grew up on a ranch and have decided that they want one of their own now."

Kylie just nodded, not sure if she was supposed to say anything when Quin looked at her. She wasn't sure she liked the gleam in his eye and wondered if he was up to something, but she didn't know him very well, so maybe she was imagining things.

"Have you told Kylie about the other families who live in Slick Rock, baby?" Quin asked Eva.

"No. We haven't had much time to talk yet."

"What other families?" Kylie asked.

Quin looked at Gray and then Pierson, and then three sets of male eyes gazed at her.

Gray cleared his throat. "There are a few polyandrous relationships in this town. Most of the people involved in ménages are our friends. We are one of eight polyandrous relationships that we know of."

"Okay, what has that got to do with me?"

"We just wanted you to be aware that not all relationships in this town are conventional," Pierson said.

"Does the thought of a woman being loved by more than one man bother you?" Quin looked like he was holding his breath, frozen in time and ready to pounce once she opened her mouth.

Kylie glared at him and let fly. "I can't believe you would ask me that." Before she knew what she was doing, she pushed back from the table and rose to her feet. "If I had a problem with what you were doing, do you think I would be here, ready to be a bridesmaid in your wedding? I don't give a fuck how you live your lives. As far as I am concerned, live and let live as long as everyone is happy and no one gets hurt. I can see how much you all love Eva and she loves you. That's all that matters to me."

Kylie stormed from the kitchen and glanced around. Whoa. Had she actually just gone off on Quin like that? She needed to get some real sleep soon, because she was losing it. Knowing Eva would come after her and not wanting to face her friend after making such a fool of herself, Kylie headed outside to walk off her aggravation, hoping to buy herself some time to pull it together. Before her tear-filled eyes could adjust to the darkness outside, she was already making her way down the front steps and heading toward the road. She didn't see the hulking figure in front of her until it was too late. Her breath left her lungs in an "oomph" as her chest connected with a rock-hard torso. Her lungs ached and burned when she couldn't take another breath. If she had been able to breathe, she would have let loose with a scream loud enough to wake the dead. Fear skittered up her spine and adrenaline spiked in her blood. Her vision grew dark from lack of oxygen, and if it hadn't been for firm hands grabbing her upper arms, she would have fallen back onto her ass. No matter how hard she tried to inhale, no air expanded her lungs. Tears streamed down her face and dripped off her jaw.

Large, warm hands caressed her back and a deep voice spoke calmly to her. "Just relax, sugar. You'll get air in a minute. Don't fight it. You'll be fine. I'm sorry I ran into you and hurt you. I wasn't looking where I was going. Shh, don't tense, I've got you."

Her tense muscles relaxed when she realized it wasn't who she had immediately thought it was. If Kylie hadn't been fighting for breath she might have shivered at the sound of that deep, masculine voice washing over her. As it was, her nipples were already hardening and she mentally cursed her body's reaction to a stranger. Another set of hands landed on her shoulders and began kneading the tight muscles. Finally, Kylie was able to fill her lungs with life-giving oxygen, and she began breathing normally again.

Sidestepping the men surrounding her, she backed up until she could see them. Her eyes had adjusted to the darkness and she was able to make out three hulking brutes watching her intently.

"Who are you?" she asked. "What are you doing here?"

The tallest and bulkiest of them stepped forward. "I'm Xavier Badon and these are my brothers, Lachlan and William. And you are?"

"Kylie Mailing." Kylie headed toward the front door, making sure she skirted the three men so she wouldn't touch them. Just as she reached for the door, it was flung open.

"Kylie, are you all right? What was that all…" Eva paused just after she flicked the porch light on and saw the men behind Kylie. "Xavier, Lachlan, Will, it's good to see you. I thought you weren't arriving until tomorrow."

"Hey, sweetie." Lachlan stepped around Kylie as she moved inside the entrance and swept Eva up into his arms, hugged her tight, and planted a kiss on her lips.

"Get your hands off my woman right now!" Quin roared, causing Kylie to jump. She edged further away from the angry-looking dominant man.

When hands once more gripped her shoulders, Kylie looked behind her to find herself staring into deep blue eyes. "Don't worry, baby. Quin's not angry. He's just playing along with Lachlan." Xavier dug his fingers into her tight muscles.

Kylie shrugged, hoping he'd take the hint and release her, but instead his hands clasped her tighter for a moment before dropping down to his sides. As he moved to stand beside her, her breathing escalated when she felt the heat coming from his body. Being surreptitious, she looked up from beneath lowered eyelashes to see him no more than half a finger length from her. If she shifted even slightly, his arm would brush against hers.

"You are such a tease and a flirt, Lachlan Badon." Eva slapped him on the shoulder as he lowered her to her feet.

"I can't help it when I'm in the presence of a pretty lady."

Kylie watched as the men slapped each other on the backs and then kissed Eva lingeringly on the lips until Pierson stepped in and pulled his fiancée into his side, giving his cousins a mock scowl.

She walked toward Kylie, took her hand, and then introduced her. "This is my best friend, Kylie Mailing." Eva tightened her grip when Kylie tried to pull away and then Eva turned toward the kitchen. "Come on into the kitchen and I'll get you something to drink. Have you had dinner?"

"Yeah, thanks, honey, but we stopped off at the diner before arriving here," Xavier said.

Kylie once again tried to escape Eva's clutches, but her friend looked at her through narrowed eyes and continued pulling her along behind her. Although she knew that Eva and her men had visited Dallas a few months ago and had time with the Badon cousins, she didn't feel comfortable in a room full of such big, brawny, handsome men. She wanted to excuse herself saying that they all needed time to catch up with each other, but she didn't think that Eva would let her get away with that, so she stayed quiet.

"At least let me get you men something to drink," Eva said as they entered the kitchen.

Xavier grinned. "I can't say no to that."

Kylie helped Eva prepare the drinks and felt eyes on her as she worked. The hair on her nape prickled and when she looked over her shoulder, all three of the Badon cousins were eying her body.

Eva sidled up to her and said for her ears alone, "What's going on, Kylie?"

"I don't know what you mean."

"Don't give me that bullshit," Eva whispered through clenched teeth. "I wasn't born yesterday. I saw the way you stormed out of the house. Now, start spilling your guts."

Kylie glanced quickly over her shoulder once more and was relieved to see that the men were engaged in conversation and were no longer looking at her.

She leaned back against the countertop. "I'm just tired." She tried once more to dissemble, but the determined glare Eva gave her let her know she wasn't about to wriggle off the hook. "Okay. Okay. Don't get your panties in a twist."

"Start talking, girlfriend! I know damn well there is something going on with you. You look like you haven't slept in months. You've lost so much weight you look almost gaunt, and I've been trying to get you to move here for the last six months, but you always had an excuse as to why you wanted to stay in Sheridan. Fess up, Kylie."

Kylie rubbed a hand over her aching forehead and sighed. "My life is in danger." She quickly placed her hand over her friend's mouth before she could screech and draw attention to them. Eva's face paled and then she gave her a slight nod to let her know she had her shock under control. She slowly removed her hand and stepped back again.

"Why? How?" Eva whispered urgently.

Kylie became aware of the silence in the room and tried not to blanch when she half turned to see what the men were doing. Six pairs of eyes were pinned to her and Eva.

"Eva, are you okay, darling?" Gray's eyes moved from Kylie to Eva and back again.

"I'm fine."

"What's going on?" Quin asked.

"Uh." Kylie stalled as her mind raced from one lie to another until she snagged on the only thing that would account for Eva's shock. "One of our friends is sick." She made sure not to look at anyone as she lied. Eva had always told her she couldn't lie worth a damn and now was probably no exception. She felt really bad for lying about something like that, but she didn't want anyone knowing her business.

"I'm sorry to hear that." Pierson's voice drew her gaze for a moment and then she turned her back on the men and faced Eva and mouthed, *"I'll tell you later."*

"Who is sick?" Quin questioned.

Eva said, "Sarah" at the same time Kylie said, "Louise."

Kylie felt her face heat, and she knew from experience that, considering her pale complexion, her cheeks were likely as red as her hair.

"Hmm," Quin murmured.

"I'm really tired after traveling so long today," Kylie said as she moved quickly toward the door. "I think I'll go to bed. Good night."

Kylie rushed down the hall and into her bedroom. Once the door was closed behind her, she leaned against the wood and groaned. Quin was probably grilling Eva right now about her lie. There was no way those men out there were going to let her get away without explaining. Not unless she refused point-blank to talk. *Yes! That's what I'll do. I'll tell them to mind their own damn business.*

Chapter Two

Fifteen minutes later, her bedroom door opened and Eva entered. Kylie was sitting on the bed, leaning against the headboard with a book in her hand, trying to appear relaxed. It didn't matter that she hadn't read more than five words before her mind began to wander. She just hoped she appeared as calm as she tried to portray.

"Kylie?" Eva sat down on the edge of the bed and waited for her to explain.

"I'm sorry I lost it before. I'll apologize to your men tomorrow."

Eva waved her hand in the air. "Don't worry about it. They can see how stressed you are." After a pause she asked, "Why is your life in danger?"

Kylie clutched her hands together and gripped her fingers so hard they began to ache. "I witnessed a crime."

"What sort of crime?"

"Rape and assault."

"Shit. No wonder you look so tired. You aren't sleeping, are you?"

"No." Kylie sighed and pushed the tips of her fingers into her closed eyelids, trying to relieve the ache behind them, again. Not that it did any good.

"Do you want to talk about it?"

Kylie shook her head but then changed to nodding. She took a deep breath and began talking. "Two weeks ago, I was working late into the night at the desk in my bedroom. I couldn't sleep so decided I may as well do something constructive and transcribe some medical notes.

"I heard what I thought was a man's muffled scream and pushed the curtains aside to peer out the window into the back alley. I didn't think I was visible, since the light in my room was off, but it turned out the light from my computer screen must have been enough to illuminate my face. A man was raping a younger man, and after he'd finished he beat him so bad." Kylie shuddered as the images flashed across her mind again. Every time she closed her eyes she saw that bastard violating the smaller man and then beating him half to death.

"I called the cops, but he must have heard them coming. Just before he took off running, he looked up and stared right at me. He made a slashing motion with his finger across his throat in warning and then disappeared."

Kylie hadn't even realized she was crying until Eva reached out and wiped the tears from her face. Then her friend pulled her into her arms and held her while she cried. When her tumultuous storm finally abated, she released her and sat back.

"Did the police catch him?"

"No," Kylie croaked. "The police took my statement and the next day I went into the precinct and worked with their artist, but they haven't been able to find him. The fucker doesn't have a record, the DNA the authorities took from the victim didn't match up to anything on their database, and the victim isn't talking. From what the police have said, he may well know who hurt him but is either too scared to press charges or doesn't want to relive his nightmare."

"Why do you think you're in danger?"

"I've had threatening letters. I've handed them over to the police but they weren't able to get any prints or DNA from them. He must have come back and found out who I was. You know that my name is on the mailbox in the foyer like everyone else who lives in my building. He had to have come in and got my name and then looked up my phone number. The bastard had to be wearing gloves. I have been too scared to go outside and when I needed something I ordered it online and had it delivered. When I called the cops about the letters they were kind enough to send someone over to pick them up. I've also had phone calls in the middle of the night."

"What?" Eva paused to swallow as if she had a lump in her throat. "What do they say?"

"That's just it. Whoever it is doesn't say anything. All I can hear is heavy breathing and then whoever it is hangs up."

"Have you told the police all this?"

"Of course I have." Kylie inhaled deeply when she heard the slight hysteria in her own voice and then released it slowly. "The cops even tapped my phone, but the prick always hangs up before the trace can be made. They can't do anything unless this asshole makes a move. Until then, their hands are tied."

"Fuck."

"Exactly." Kylie flung her book aside and stood. "The cops suggested I go and stay with friends or relatives for a while. I decided to do one better and move. At least this dipshit doesn't know where I am anymore."

"I'm glad you're here. My men can protect you and so can their cousins. You'll be safe here, Kylie."

"I can't stay here, Eva. If this asshole finds me, I'll be putting all of you in danger."

"No, you won't. I'll be on my three-week honeymoon in five days' time. There is no way I'm letting you leave. If this guy manages to find you, what are you going to do when he comes after you?"

"I can look after myself, I have for years."

"Damn it, Kylie. What if he comes after you with a gun? You can't dodge bullets and you aren't bulletproof."

"You think I don't know that?" Kylie wailed before taking another deep breath, trying to get her fear and emotions under control. She released it with a long, drawn-out sigh. "I'm going to find somewhere to live. I can't stay here for the rest of my life."

"No, you aren't going anywhere. I'll talk to my men. They'll figure something out."

"I don't think that's such a good idea. The more they know, the more danger they'll be in. God, Eva, I shouldn't have come here at all. I should never have accepted being your bridesmaid, but I missed you so damn much."

Eva walked up to her and wrapped her arms around her. It had been so long since she'd been held, and the offer of comfort broke down the walls she had kept herself hidden behind. Kylie was so tired she didn't know how much longer she could keep going. If she didn't get a good night's sleep soon, she was scared she was going to break.

Eva eased back and kissed Kylie on the cheek when a knock sounded on the door. Kylie turned her back as her friend went to let whoever was there in, trying to compose herself and made sure no moisture was left on her face.

"Is everything all right in here?" Quin asked, and Kylie heard the door close again.

"No," Eva replied in a croaky voice and began to explain what Kylie had witnessed.

"Fuck," Quin's footsteps sounded behind her and then she was being pulled up against a large masculine frame. Kylie wasn't attracted to Eva's men, even though she found them extremely handsome. But when Quin put his arms around her, she felt safe for the first time since she had witnessed the crime taking place, and she didn't want to let go. She'd had enough of being alone and scared, but Quin, Gray, and Pierson weren't hers and she couldn't rely on them. They would be leaving with Eva and she would have no one again.

Kylie had to shore up her defenses and stand on her own two feet. She had for a long time now, so why would today be any different?

"I'm sorry I snapped at you before."

"Don't worry about it, sweetheart. You're obviously under a lot of stress. We'll keep you safe, Kylie. I promise. Trust us to protect you," Quin murmured and kissed the top of head before releasing her.

"That's not fair to you, your brother's, or Eva. You're getting ready to get married and I don't want to interrupt your plans." She drew in a ragged breath and began to pace. "After the dress fitting tomorrow, I'm going to find a place of my own."

"No," Quin stated in a loud, cold, hard voice. "There is no fucking way you're leaving."

"You can't stop me. I'm an adult and make my own decisions," Kylie shouted and then spun away as her bedroom door was pushed open, again.

"What's going on?" Xavier asked as he took a couple of steps into the room. Kylie glanced over her shoulder and saw the rest of the men were right behind him. She turned to face them.

Xavier pinned her with his eyes and her breath hitched in her throat. He had to be around six foot five and he was solid as a rock. His muscles bulged and flexed as he crossed his arms over his massive chest and held her gaze with his blue eyes. Kylie released the breath she had been holding and hoped to God that he didn't see the way her nipples stood up and took notice. She shifted restlessly from one foot to the other and then clamped her thighs together tightly as her clit began to throb and moisture dripped from her pussy to her panties, soaking the crotch. Never had she reacted so strongly to a male as she did to this man and his brothers.

Xavier was too ruggedly masculine to be considered handsome, but boy did he have an aura of manliness she had never encountered before. If it hadn't been for his slightly too long brown hair and his full lips, which helped to soften his machismo, she may have been scared of his powerful appearance.

She was finally able to wrench her gaze from his, but she was immediately enthralled when she connected with a pair of green eyes. Lachlan was just as impressive as his brother but not as tall. He was around six four, and even though he was ripped and muscular he wasn't as big as Xavier. His hair was a deeper brown than Xavier's and shorter. And although he was handsome in a more classical way, he also had a ruggedness about him that only enhanced his good looks, making him appear just as manly as his brother. His square jaw had dark stubble, and he looked a couple of years younger than Xavier.

Kylie crossed her arms over her chest, hoping the three men who were staring at her hadn't noticed her prominent nipples, and once more shuffled on her feet. Her eyes shifted again and locked on to a pair of gray eyes staring back at her. William, or Will, as his brothers called him, had sandy-brown hair and was looking at her as if she was the last woman on Earth. He was the youngest and the shortest of the three Badon cousins, and though he was a lot leaner than his brothers, his biceps and pecs bulged as he crossed his arms over his chest.

They were three very handsome, impressive men and they got her motor revving like no other man ever had.

Kylie managed to remove her eyes from Will's, and as she did, she became aware of Quin's voice rumbling quietly as he explained why she was so upset. Once Quin finished speaking, the silence in the room was almost deafening.

Xavier stepped forward and cupped her face. "There is no way in hell you are leaving. Your life is in danger and it's our job to protect you."

"No." Kylie stepped away from him until her back connected with the wall behind her. "I'm not staying here and putting you all in danger. I couldn't live with my conscience if something happened to you. You're all just starting your lives. I'm not going to be the reason one of you ends up hurt."

"Kylie, the men of this town are very protective and dominant," Pierson said. "All we have to do is let everyone know you are in danger and they will be on the lookout for any strangers. There is no way in hell anyone will get to you if the whole town is on alert."

"You guys have enough to do and on your mind without having to worry about me. I think the best thing would be if I just leave. Don't you realize that Eva could get hurt?"

"That won't ever happen." Quin pulled Eva up against his side. "We take care of our women. This asshole after you would have to go through us before hurting either of you."

"That's just it." Kylie covered her mouth when a sob escaped. "I don't want that happening."

"We'll make sure Kylie is protected." Xavier stared at her as if daring her to refute him, but she could see by the determination in his eyes that if she argued with him, she wouldn't stand a chance in hell. And by the indomitable set of Lachlan's and Will's clenched jaws they were just as dogged of mind.

Kylie sighed and pressed her fingers to her aching eyes. She was just too tired to argue and deal with any of them right now. She'd already had one outburst tonight and she didn't want to make a fool of herself with another. "Can we talk about this in the morning? I just want to crawl into bed and sleep."

"Okay," Quin finally answered. "I can see how exhausted you are. Try to get some rest, honey. We'll see you in the morning."

Gray and Pierson sighed but left her room. Eva escaped from Quin's embrace and gave her a tight hug. "I love you like a sister, Kylie. Please don't leave?" Eva whispered for her ears alone.

"I'll think about it." She released her friend. Quin guided her from the room and she was left alone with Xavier, Lachlan, and William.

Will's voice drew her gaze. "Kylie, I know you don't know us, but we've been working as bodyguards for over eight years. We can protect you if you'll just let us."

"I–I…Shit." Kylie turned away from three piercing gazes, and even though she was no longer looking at them, she could still feel their eyes on her.

"Think about it, sugar. We'll talk to you in the morning." Lachlan and Will headed toward the door with Xavier on their heels. Xavier paused in the doorway, looking at her over his shoulder.

"This isn't over, baby."

Kylie sighed and sank down onto the edge of the bed as the door closed. Her mind and emotions were in turmoil. Even though she wanted to stay, she knew it wasn't the right thing to do. Putting everyone around her in danger wasn't conducive to her peace of mind in the least.

She undressed and pulled her sleeping shorts and T-shirt on. She knew from past experience that she would have trouble falling asleep. The violent incident was as fresh in her mind as if she had just witnessed the crime, and even though she was exhausted and her head was aching, she knew it would be hours before she finally succumbed to sleep.

She tried envisaging sitting near a brook with birds chirping around her and the sound of water gurgling over rocks but her thoughts were too scattered. She readied herself for another sleepless night, but this time it wasn't the visions of the crime she witnessed that preoccupied her mind. No, tonight she was surprised that her mind was spinning from the instant attraction she felt for the three Badon cousins. Now *that* scared the absolute shit out of her!

* * * *

Kylie was typing rapidly, her fingers flying over the keyboard of her laptop as she transcribed medical facts for a doctor. Her hands froze when she thought she heard a muffled shout. Her desk was close to her bedroom window and all she had to do was spin a little and push the curtains aside to see out into the lane beside her apartment building. Her eyes searched the alley until they lit on two male figures. One was very tall and big and the other looked to be thin and gangly. She let her eyes adjust to the dimmer light outside after looking at her bright computer monitor, and when she did, her hand flew to her mouth as she gasped.

The large man had pinned the smaller man to the ground, facedown, and had his jeans and underwear down around his ankles. And then she nearly yelled with fury when her brain finally registered what she was seeing.

Kylie's eyes glanced toward her desk and quickly grabbed her cell phone and dialed 9-1-1. When the despatcher answered, Kylie gave her name and address and reported what she was seeing. She was vaguely aware of the dispatcher saying that someone was on the way when the bastard finished raping his victim. Then Kylie watched in horror as he punched and kicked his victim until the smaller man was lying on the cold, hard concrete in the alley without moving.

She had no idea whether she had made a noise to alert the perp, but all of sudden he turned his head and looked up. Kylie couldn't see his eyes but she knew in her heart that he was looking right at her. There was a low wattage lamp ten yards from where the rapist stood and even though she could see his face, his eyes were in shadow. Just as she placed her hand against the rapid pulse in her neck, the bastard smiled at her, his white teeth seemingly bright in the darkness and then he raised his hand to his throat, placed a finger at one side of his neck and ran it across to the other. She cringed back but still couldn't seem to look away. But then he cocked his head as if listening and took off running, disappearing into the shadows at the other end of the alley and that was when she heard the distinct wail of a siren.

But then everything changed. Kylie somehow was standing in the middle of the alley, shaking fearfully. There was no lamplight and she couldn't see anything. Goose bumps and a cold sweat broke out across her skin and she clutched her cold hands into fists. She could feel his eyes on her. Turning in slow circles, she tried to find where he was hiding so she could run in the opposite direction, but he stayed elusive in the shadows. Just when she opened her mouth to scream, cold metal pressed against one side of her throat. Drawing in a gasp of breath she opened her mouth and let loose with the loudest yell she could. Her cry was cut off when the knife slid along her flesh and into her throat.

Her hands clawed at her neck and she made gurgling sounds, but her eyesight was diminishing rapidly.

Kylie knew she was dying.

Chapter Three

Xavier sat up, rolled to his feet, instantly awake, and reached for his gun, which he always placed on the bedside table, as a piercing scream rent the air. He quickly pulled his jeans on and, with gun in hand, cautiously opened his bedroom door and scanned the hallway. When he saw that it was all clear, he moved stealthily along the hallway until he reached the next bedroom door. His hand was already on the doorknob, turning it slowly when his brothers joined him. None of them spoke as he pushed the door open. Will slipped inside the bedroom quickly checking behind the door as Lachlan raced to the bathroom across the other side of the room.

After he and his brothers ascertained that there was no danger, Xavier approached the bed where Kylie was shifting restlessly. Just as he reached her side another bloodcurdling scream left her mouth and then she was grabbing at her neck and making a funny gurgling sound as if she couldn't breathe.

Will switched on the bedside lamp on the other side of the bed, illuminating Kylie in the dim light.

"Jesus!" Xavier reached down and pulled her hands away from her throat. She'd left red welted scratch marks on her neck. "Kylie, wake up."

A tortured moan left her mouth and then was she fighting him, trying to get away. Another bloodcurdling scream rent the air, making the hair on his nape stand on end. Xavier hated seeing her tortured in her sleep and didn't want her hurting herself as she tried to fight off her nightmarish assailant, so he did the only thing he could think of. He covered her body with his, making sure not to crush her with his weight but applying enough pressure so she couldn't move anymore. He brought her arms up above her head, pinning them to the mattress while quietly talking to her.

"Kylie, you're safe. It's only a dream, baby. Come on now. Open those pretty eyes for me." Xavier felt the instant he got through to her. She stopped trying to thrash beneath him, and even though her body was still taut and shaking, her breathing changed. Instead of the gurgling panting sounds she had been making, she gulped in great gasps of air and then her eyelids slid up and he stared into her pretty green eyes.

He slowly released her arms, and using his elbows propped the top half of his body up from hers before carefully lifting his pelvis away from her lower half, hoping she hadn't noticed his burgeoning cock. He then wiped the tears from her cheeks with his thumb.

"What's going on?" Quin's deep, gravelly voice pulled Xavier from the trance he hadn't been aware he was in.

With great care, Xavier rolled off of Kylie and sat up next to her as Lachlan explained what had happened.

Quin walked further into the room and stopped at the end of the bed, looking at Kylie, who was taking great pains not to look any of them in the eye as she clutched the covers to her chest. "Are you okay, Kylie?"

"Yes," she answered with a cracked voice, and then she cleared her throat. "I'm sorry I woke you all."

"Don't worry about that, honey. I'm just glad you're all right." Quin eyed Xavier and then his brothers, giving them a narrow-eyed stare before turning his gaze back to Kylie. "Do you want to talk about your nightmare?"

"No!" she replied emphatically then replied again with a palliated tone. "No, thank you."

Quin sighed and turned toward the door. "We're here if you want to talk, honey. All you have to do is come to one of us and we'll listen."

"Thanks, but I'm fine."

"Okay, I'll see you in the morning." Quin gave Xavier another measured stare. "Try to get some more rest, Kylie."

Xavier didn't speak until Quin disappeared from sight. He knew that stare was a warning to him and his brothers, but Xavier would never do anything to hurt Kylie on purpose. He supposed if Quin's fiancée's friend was under his care, then he would also make sure she was protected and taken care of, so he knew where his cousin was coming from. But he was still a little pissed off, because Quin knew damn well he would never hurt a woman or child. Pushing his irritation with his cousin aside, he finally turned back toward Kylie. Her breathing was still elevated, but it was slowing. By the white-knuckled grip she had on the top of the covers, he would bet if she released them he would be able to see her hands visibly shaking.

"Are you sure you're okay, beautiful?" Will took a seat on the end of the bed near Kylie's feet and then placed a hand on her shin over the blankets.

"Yes, I'm good." Kylie stuck her chin slightly into the air as if shoring up her defenses. The action more telling than words, her next statement confirmed his suspicions. "You can leave now."

Xavier didn't want to leave. He wanted lie down beside her, pull her into his arms and hold her all night long. With a mental frown, he realized he'd never wanted to do that before. He and his brothers had gone through their share of women over the years, but they were sick and tired of emotionless sex. They had decided around six months ago that they wanted to get back into ranching, and after much deliberation on their part, they had gone to see a financial advisor and found out that they had more than enough cash to pay for what they wanted outright. But Xavier had wanted to have another few months' savings up their sleeve before biting the bullet and resigning from their security jobs. Now that they were ready to buy an operation and were out of such dangerous work, they were also ready to settle down and have a relationship with one woman.

He and his siblings had always been attracted to the same type of women and had ended up sharing a few times. After the third such session, they had sat and talked for hours and decided that maybe they would want to share a wife, too. Xavier had thought that idea had been a pipe dream. That was until Quin, Gray, and Pierson had moved to Slick Rock, Colorado, and found the love of their life. But what had clinched the deal for him was the fact that his cousins' relationship wasn't the only ménage, and that unconventional relationships were expected and accepted in the small, rural town. That wasn't to say there weren't some folks who baulked at such things, but mostly the unconventional was accepted as the norm and anyone heard disparaging or making vilifying comments was ostracized, and if they owned a business, they were boycotted until they went bankrupt and left town.

Xavier wanted to explore the attraction he and his brothers had toward Kylie, but he wasn't sure what her take on a polyandrous relationship was, so they would have to start off slow. All things considered, Kylie had enough on her shoulders without him or his brothers adding to her worries. He wasn't sure what to do at the moment, but there was one thing he was certain of, and that was that there was no way Kylie was leaving and putting herself in more danger.

Xavier rolled to his feet with a sigh and then turned to look at Kylie again. She looked so lost and scared in the bed, but there wasn't a damn thing he could do about it, at least not yet. He and his brothers were going to have to talk and plan. He wanted Kylie to be able to come to him, Lachlan, or Will if she needed to talk things out, but first they had to ease her into a relationship.

"If you need anything, beautiful, all you have to do is give a yell," Will said before he left. Lachlan didn't say anything. He gave one last longing look toward the bed and followed Will out.

"We'd like to be able to help you, Kylie," Xavier said as he paused in the doorway. "We have the expertise to keep you safe. Think about it."

Xavier closed the door quietly behind him and headed to the kitchen. He wasn't surprised to see Quin and Gray already sitting at the table, talking quietly while Lachlan and Will made three more cups of coffee.

With coffee now in hand, Xavier eased himself into a seat as did his brothers. He should have known Quin would get right to the point.

"What are your intentions?"

"Fuck, Quin, you don't mince words, do you?"

"Never have and never will." Quin leaned back in his chair.

"We want her," Lachlan stated abruptly.

"Yeah, I kinda figured. Explain."

"You know we want to have our own ranch," Xavier paused and took a sip of coffee while he gathered his thoughts. "We want a woman to share our beds."

"For how long?" Quin asked, staring at him through narrowed eyes.

"Permanently," Xavier answered and watched the tension slowly drain from his cousin's muscles.

"She's going to give you a fight."

"Yeah, I know." Xavier sighed.

"There is no way she's leaving without us exploring the attraction between us first," Will said, putting in his two cents.

Xavier glanced at his brother. Usually Will was most easygoing of them all. For him to make a statement like that, he had to be very attracted to Kylie, too. *Thank you, God.* He hadn't had time to speak to his brothers to find out how they felt about pursuing Kylie. Obviously he'd seen how physically drawn to her they were, but Will's statement just confirmed that he was on board. He glanced toward Lach and received a nod.

"It just so happens that Eva told me Kylie has leased out her apartment in Sheridan and is all set to find a place to lease here."

"Does this decision have anything to do with this fucker stalking her?"

"Yes, although Eva has been working on Kylie for about six months, trying to get her to move and be closer to her. She's running scared as she has every right to, and from what I gather, the law in her hometown suggested she might want to stay with relatives or friends, since it's uncertain who this fucker is."

"Why haven't they got anything on him?" Xavier leaned forward in his chair.

"It appears that this was his first offense. DNA was taken from the victim, but there was nothing in the police database to connect him to, and the letters he sent to Kylie were all clean. According to Eva, and this is from Kylie, the cops have nothing and can't do a thing until this prick makes a move."

"Do they know what he looks like?"

"Only the description Kylie gave the police artist."

"I want a copy of that picture."

Quin nodded. "I'll contact the sheriff's department in the morning and let them know what we're dealing with. Between Luke Sun-Walker and Damon Osborn, as well as the deputies, we should be able to get some information."

Quin and Gray stood and stretched. "We can go visit the sheriff while the two girls have their dress fitting. That way Kylie won't be aware that we are doing everything we can to protect her."

"She's just going to have to accept that we want to help her. Her safety is paramount," Lach said in a firm voice. Xavier and Will nodded in agreement.

Gray snorted. "Good luck with that." Gray and Quin headed back to bed, leaving Xavier and his brothers alone.

"So, how the hell are we going to woo that woman into our life and beds and keep her safe?" Will asked.

"Let's get her used to us being around first," Lach said. "If we can keep here her close and protect her, then we have a chance of wooing her."

"That little filly is a skittish as if she were a mare facing a rattle snake." Xavier sipped from his mug.

"It's understandable that she is wary. Look at what she has had to deal with over the last couple of weeks." Will leaned his elbows on the table and wrapped his hands around his now-empty coffee mug.

"We can't do anything else tonight. Let's head back to bed and get a few hours of shut-eye." Xavier headed out. "Hopefully in the morning things will look a whole lot brighter."

Xavier paused outside Kylie's bedroom door. There was a strip of light glowing under the door and before he knew that he was going to do it, he had raised his hand to knock. He hesitated before his knuckles connected with the wood. If he knocked and she was asleep, he would feel really bad for disturbing her. She may have left the light on after the nightmare she'd had. But she could also being lying in her bed wide awake, too scared to go back to sleep. From the look of the dark smudges beneath her eyes and the hollowness of her cheeks, she'd already suffered a lot of sleep loss. Probably her appetite had suffered, too. Women were strange creatures. Whenever their emotions were in turmoil, they either ate, trying to gain false comfort, or their appetite diminished totally.

Xavier vowed that starting tomorrow morning, he and his brothers were going to take care of Kylie and make sure she ate whether she wanted to or not. The last thing she needed was to get sick on top of everything else. She was such a delicate little thing. Although she was just shy of the average height for a woman, standing at around five foot five, she was willow thin and delicate, but showed signs of having curves before her loss of appetite had set in, and he wanted to run his hands all over her body, shaping every dip and hollow he found. He'd noticed how small her wrists were and her skin was so pale it was almost lucent. Her deep, red, shoulder-length hair only seemed to enhance her delicate features and her green eyes seemed to draw him in whenever she met his gaze. Yet there wasn't one single freckle marring her beautiful face. Not that any sun spots would have detracted from her looks. In fact, he had a feeling no matter what Kylie looked like, he would still feel the deep attraction he had toward her.

Kylie Mailing seemed to have a spine of steel but underneath the backbone was a deeply vulnerable and lonely woman.

At the sound of his brothers approaching, he sighed longingly, lowered his hand that was still hovering near the door, turned on his heel, and hurried into his bedroom. He wouldn't have cared if Will and Lach had caught him staring at the door in a trance. He and his brothers really didn't need words to know what the others were thinking. They had lived and worked together for so long they could sometimes finish each other's sentences or answer a question before it was voiced. They were as connected as some twins and triplets seemed to be. They knew each other too well to not understand how each of their thought process worked, to a certain degree.

Because of their compatibility and understanding of each other, they had been the best bodyguard team at the security company and their bosses had kicked up quite a stink when they had resigned. The director of the company had even offered them double their already more than generous salary, but he and his brothers had had enough traveling and living such a lonely life. No amount of money could make up for a life without a loving woman.

Now all he and his brothers had to do was convince Kylie that she was the woman for them and they were the men for her.

Now how did that saying go? *"Life isn't meant to be easy."* That was an understatement if ever he heard one.

Considering the quick temper he'd already seen in her, there might be a fine line between impressing her and pissing her off. He could only hope to figure out how to walk that line.

Chapter Four

"Oh, my God, Eva, you look absolutely stunning," Kylie said with a hitch in her breath.

"Do you really think so?" Eva asked as she turned this way and that, looking in the huge mirror on the back wall of the bridal shop.

"That dress is going to knock your fiancés on their asses." Kylie admired the simple yet elegant dress Eva had chosen as her wedding gown. It was strapless, with the bodice shaped firmly over her breasts and ribs, but instead of the skirt flaring out over her hips, it was fitted and the long skirt was nearly pencil thin with a small two-foot train trailing off the back. There were no frilly adornments at all. It was plain and simple yet beautifully elegant, just like her friend.

"What shoes are you going to wear? And how are you going to wear your leg brace?"

"My shoes are over there," Eva pointed to a box off to the right. "Can you get them for me?"

"Sure." Kylie retrieved the box and then passed the low-heeled white shoes to Eva and held her elbow while she balanced to put them on her feet.

"I'm not wearing my brace. I don't think one day is going to hurt too much. Besides, if I end up with a cramp, I will have three hot, sexy husbands to help me out." Eva gave her a lascivious wink and then laughed.

"You are so bad." Kylie stepped back once more to view her friend in her wedding finery. "You're stunning, girlfriend. Those men won't know what hit them."

"Okay. Can you unzip me?"

Kylie helped Eva out of her dress, and when her friend was once more wearing her jeans and T-shirt and had handed her dress and shoes off to the sales assistant to be packed up, she turned and eyed her up and down.

"It's your turn now. Come with me." Eva grabbed her hand and led her a few paces toward a rack with dresses hanging on it. Obviously, Eva knew what she wanted, because she didn't waste any time pulling a green dress from the rack. "Try this on."

Kylie held the dress up and barely held in her gasp of awe. The dress was gorgeous. It was simple and also strapless like Eva's, but it was also very daring. She eyed the heart-shaped bodice and the hole in the center beneath the breast line. The dress was open on both sides as well as the middle, and a slit ran up the length of the right side of the skirt.

"Shit, are you trying to give me pneumonia?"

"Stop your quibbling and try it on. If you don't like how it looks or feels after you try it, I'll let you pick out something else."

Kylie eyed the dress dubiously, but she wanted to make Eva happy. So with a resigned sigh, she headed to the fitting room. A couple of minutes later, Kylie was staring at a stranger. The woman in the mirror was pretty, almost beautiful and not someone she had ever seen before. Pale skin on her sides showed through, contrasting nicely with the emerald-green silk of the dress. The strategically placed hole in the fabric showed even more skin to just above her panty line, and when she moved, the slit in the skirt revealed even more flesh.

"Have you got it on yet? I've found some matching shoes." Eva called through the curtain. "Kylie?"

Kylie gave the woman in the mirror one last look and the opened the curtain. She waited with bated breath while Eva looked her over.

"Oh my God. You are the most stunning woman I have ever seen. Xavier, Lach, and Will won't be able to take their eyes off of you."

"What?" Kylie squawked and then cleared her throat.

"Oh, come on. Don't tell me you haven't seen the way they all look at you."

"Don't start, Eva." Kylie snatched the emerald-green high heels from her friend's hand and bent to put them on.

"Make sure you don't bend over like that on the day of the wedding, because you will have every male eye pinned to that hole in the dress, wondering if your boobs will fall out." Eva chuckled.

"They won't. I already checked. The support in the bodice will prevent me from flashing anyone." Kylie straightened up and looked at Eva. "There is no way in hell I'm getting involved with anyone."

"Do you like the dress?" Eva asked.

Kylie narrowed her eyes and stared at her friend. She knew damn well that Eva was ignoring her last statement.

"Yes. I would feel more comfortable if there were a little more to it, though."

"Kylie, you have never seen how pretty you are. I wish you would see yourself the way I see you. You are gorgeous, girl, and will have every single man at the wedding vying for your attention."

"I don't want a man in my life, Eva. God, I have a lunatic stalking me. The last thing I need or want is a relationship right now."

"You want them just as much as they want you. Did you think I didn't notice the way you were looking at them over breakfast? The sexual tension between you four was so thick I could have cut it with my knife."

"Just because I'm attracted to them doesn't mean a thing." Kylie began to carefully remove the dress with the curtain still open so she could see Eva as they talked. "They are arrogant, conceited, bossy assholes, and I don't want anything to do with them."

"You're lying to yourself, Kylie." Eva sighed as she took the dress from her. "They may seem arrogant and domineering, but they are just what you need. If it hadn't been for those three men cajoling and pushing you, you wouldn't have eaten your breakfast. Do you think I didn't notice you hardly ate anything last night? That you just pushed your food around your plate pretending to eat? You have lost too much weight, girlfriend. I'm worried about you. You have dark smudges beneath your eyes from lack of sleep and your ribs are poking through your skin. You're beginning to look anorexic."

Kylie sighed but didn't argue with Eva. What could she say to the truth? Kylie had lost just over ten pounds and although she had been healthy, she'd always been on the lighter side of her ideal weight for her height. She'd been living on fear and nerves too long, and it was starting to show. Maybe now that she was away from her hometown and that asshole, she could begin to relax a little. But deep down she knew he would catch up to her. Somehow, someway, her life was in danger and there wasn't a damn thing she could do about it.

* * * *

Will studied the sketch the police artist in Sheridan had compiled from the information Kylie had given him, and then handed it to Xavier, frustrated that Kylie hadn't been able to see the shape of his eyes or their color.

After breakfast, Will, Xavier, and Lachlan as well as their cousins went down to the sheriff's department to visit Damon Osborn and Luke Sun-Walker to see what information they could dig up about Kylie's stalker. What worried Will the most was that if the prick managed to track Kylie to Slick Rock, she may not recognize him and she would be in danger.

"Has any information been found on this fucker?" Lach asked Sheriff Luke Sun-Walker.

"No."

"I've done a complete nationwide data check," Sheriff Damon Osborn said. "No alerts came up."

"Fuck." Will burst to his feet and began to pace in the sheriff's office. "I hate this shit. Surely someone somewhere knows who he is.

A man doesn't change his spots overnight. He had to have broken the law before now."

"Surely there have been other reports of rape, right, Sheriff?"

"Women, yes, but men is another story." Luke sighed and leaned back in his chair. "I'll go through the database and see if there have been any reports on rape against males, but you and I both know that not all crimes are reported.

"From the description on the bottom of the artist's depiction, the perpetrator is one large, mean son of a bitch. Ms. Mailing's description was also a little vague. She couldn't see his eyes or really tell what color his hair was. Without more precise information this is like looking for a needle in a haystack."

"I would suggest you stay close to your woman." Damon tapped a couple of keys on his keyboard and then looked at each of them. "Stay vigilant and don't let her out of your sight."

"Easier said than done," Xavier muttered.

"God, I'm so glad we are past the wooing stage with Eva." Quin smirked.

"Felicity gave Tom, Billy, and me a run for our money." Luke smiled.

"Rachel kept Tyson, Sam, and me on our toes, too," Damon said.

"Just make sure you go slowly with her," Gray suggested. "If you push her too far, I can see her running."

"Okay, let's go join our women for lunch at the diner." Lach folded the picture and put it in his pocket.

"Don't worry too much about Kylie." Luke stood and shook his hand. "I've already got all the men in town on alert. If any strangers show up in Slick Rock, we'll be ready."

"Thanks, Luke, Damon." Will shook Damon's hand and headed out. His brothers and cousins joined him after saying good-bye to the law officers.

They were already waiting at the diner when the women arrived. Will looked Kylie over and was pleased to see her safe and sound. He hated to see her looking so tense and tired, but there wasn't really anything he could do about it. At least not yet. What he wouldn't give to have her in his arms with her naked body along his. He pushed his thoughts aside when he noticed Kylie's frown and the way she was looking out the window as she followed Eva to the booth.

He scanned the area but couldn't see anything, so he turned his gaze back to Kylie. Her face was paler than normal and he wondered if she was feeling sick. Eva sat down in the booth across from theirs with her men, and when he saw Kylie eying the space next to Pierson, he rose to his feet and maneuvered around until he blocked that seat. Kylie had no choice but to sit with him and his brothers.

She gave him a glare and practically threw herself down on the seat in a fit of pique and then snatched up the menu and pointedly ignored him and his brothers. Will glanced at his brothers and saw the humor in their eyes, just as he tried to school his own features, so as to not upset Kylie, his brothers did the same.

The waitress approached their table and stopped with her pen and pad in hand. "What will you have?" she asked.

Will, Xavier, and Lach ordered and waited while Kylie did the same. He was about to step in when she ordered a salad, but Xavier beat him to it. "And another burger with the lot."

The waitress moved across to the other booth and Will waited for the explosion, counting in his head, wondering how long it would take.

One. Two. Three. Four. Five. Six...

"Just who the hell do you think you are?" Kylie snapped. "I'm a grown woman and have been taking care of myself for a long time. I don't need you or your Neanderthal brothers taking over my life."

"Then start acting like an adult and I will treat you like one," Xavier said in a cold, hard voice.

"Xavier." Will glared at his brother.

Kylie made a growling noise in her throat and then turned toward him. "Let me out."

"No," Will replied calmly.

"Look, you arrogant ass, I need to use the ladies' room. So unless you want to be cleaning up a puddle off the floor, you will let me out this instant."

Will eyed the furious woman beside him. He didn't think she really needed the bathroom, but he wasn't about to stop her going if that's what she wanted. Beneath that furious glare he could see desire and her need to ignore it. Kylie Mailing wasn't only running from the asshole after her, she was running from him and his brothers as well as herself. But that was about to change. He wasn't going to let her ignore the feelings she had for him and his brothers. Usually he was the patient one out of the three of them, but this time he wasn't about to hang back. It was too important that he and his brothers get Kylie within the circle of their arms where they could keep her safe from her stalker and also from herself.

She needed them more than she knew.

The food was brought out and still there was no sight of Kylie. She had been gone for nearly ten minutes and he was beginning to get worried. Trying to act casual so Eva wouldn't notice that her friend was no longer sitting down, he sauntered toward the back hall, where the restrooms were situated. Will knocked but was met with no immediate reply. He put his ear to the door and was ready to knock again, this time harder, when he heard the sounds of muffled sobs coming from the other side. That was more than he could stand to hear. He flung open the door, and what he saw tore his heart out. Kylie was sitting on the floor against the wall underneath the pair of hand dryers, with her knees drawn up and her arms wrapped around her legs. Her head was resting on her knees and her hair was obscuring her face. Her shoulders were shaking and she was gasping for breath.

Will hurried over and sat on the floor beside her. Kylie was so caught up in her misery that she didn't even notice, or if she did she didn't show it. He wrapped an arm around her shoulders and another around her tiny waist and scooped her up and onto his lap. She looked up for a second and then she buried her face against his chest. Her whole body was trembling from her efforts to hold her emotions in.

"Let it out, sweetheart." He ran a soothing hand up and down her back. "I'll hold you and keep you safe."

Will continued to hold her while she cried, and finally her trembling abated and he suspected so did her tears. Finally she lifted her head and swiped at the moisture on her cheeks with the backs of her hands.

"Are you okay, honey?"

"Yeah," she answered on a hiccup. "I'm sorry. I don't normally cry."

"Kylie, don't you dare be sorry. You've been living under a lot of stress and not sleeping. It's all taking a toll and has to compound and come out sometime."

"I'm sorry I snapped at you before."

"Don't worry about it, sweet thang. We all need to let off steam now and then."

Kylie must have realized where she was and tilted her head slightly before asking, "What are you doing in the ladies' bathroom?"

"I was worried when you didn't come back after a bit, so I decided to check on you."

"Oh." She tried pushing the arm around her waist away, but he was having none of that. Not when he had finally got her where he wanted her.

"Are you hungry?" Will asked. He'd intended the double entendre, but realized that she hadn't caught it once she answered him with a slight smile.

"Yes, actually I am."

"Good." Will decided to let her see how hungry he was. "So am I."

He lowered his head and brushed his lips back and forth over hers. At first she stiffened in his arms, but as he continued to ply light kisses on her mouth, she relaxed against him. He slid his tongue across the seam of her mouth and she opened up to him on a sigh. That was all he had been waiting for, a green light from her to take the kiss deeper. He thrust his tongue inside and tasted her. She was everything he thought she would be and a hell of a lot more. She was home and hearth and desire and sex all rolled into one slim package.

He groaned into her mouth and slid his tongue along hers. She kissed him back just as voraciously, and she shifted on his lap, making his half-hard cock suddenly stiffen completely. Without breaking the kiss, he shifted his hands to her waist and lifted her until she was straddling his hips. Her soft breasts smashed up against his chest and her hard little nipples stabbed him.

Will knew he couldn't take this any further. He was already in danger of coming in his pants, since he could feel the moist heat of her pussy against his hard cock through the fabric of their jeans, but this wasn't the place to continue seducing her. They were in the women's restroom in the diner, for God's sake, and anyone could walk in at any moment. He began to run his hands up and down her back and arms, which she had linked around his neck, and then eased the hungry kisses down until he was sipping at her lips. Finally he pulled his mouth away from hers and stared into her passion-glazed green eyes.

She was a stunning woman and had no idea how much she affected him and his brothers. Her face and neck were also flushed a red hue and he wondered how far down that flush went.

"Why did you do that?"

"You and I both know that this attraction between us is a two-way street, sweetheart. Don't you dare say that you didn't enjoy that as much as I did!"

Kylie pushed against his shoulder and scrambled to her feet. She kept her face turned away from him, but he could see her profile in the mirror on the wall, and he gained his feet with a sigh.

"Look, just because I am attracted to you doesn't give you license to paw me whenever you want," Kylie snapped. "I have enough to worry about without dealing with you and your domineering brothers. Just leave me the hell alone."

Kylie pulled the door to the bathroom open and stormed out without a backward glance. But Will didn't worry too much about her dramatic exit, as one thought dominated his mind. She was attracted to him, better yet, to all three of them. He couldn't wait to deliver the good news to his brothers.

Chapter Five

The days leading up to the wedding flew past. Kylie had worked really hard at avoiding the three Badon cousins, but whenever they were nearby, they took every opportunity they could to touch her in some way. She was getting mighty sick of being pawed.

You're lying to yourself, girl. You want them as much as they seem to want you.

Kylie sighed and scanned the properties to lease in the local paper. Since Slick Rock was such a small town, there wasn't much. She had found an apartment and a room to rent with two other girls, but as far as she was concerned, sharing was definitely out. If the rapist who had been stalking her ever found her, she would be putting other people in danger, and she wasn't about to let that happen. It was bad enough that she was still living in Eva's spare room, putting her and her men in the line of fire, let alone anyone who had no clue as to what was going on or could go down. She picked up her cell phone but hesitated with her fingers over the number pad. Did she really want to be alone and scared?

Kylie had lived alone for the last few years and the last four days spent with Eva and her men had pushed her worries to the back of her mind. Yes, even the Badon cousins had had a hand in relieving her anxiety somewhat. Just as she was about to start dialing, a knock sounded at her door.

"Kylie, are you ready yet?" Eva poked her head around the edge of the door and Kylie saw that her face had a light application of makeup.

She glanced at the time on her phone and saw that it was nearly time to leave. "Shit." She flung the paper aside and raced toward the bathroom. "I'll be ready in ten."

"Okay, but why don't you get a lift with Xavier and his brothers? My guys and I have to be at the restaurant to greet the other guests very soon."

Kylie hesitated at the bathroom door. As much as she wanted to ask Eva to wait for her, she couldn't. That wouldn't be fair to her friend and her fiancés. With a resigned sigh, she gave Eva a nod of her head and rushed into the bathroom. After the fastest shower on record, she donned her underwear and then applied a bit of makeup. She was glad she'd had the foresight to wash her hair that morning, and since she had planned to leave it down, all she did was give it a good brushing. She opened the closet, grabbed the black dress she planned to wear, pulled the zipper up the back with a little difficulty, and then slipped her feet into her black high-heeled shoes. She was just reaching for her purse and a wrap when someone knocked on the door.

"Are you ready, Kylie?" Lachlan's voice came through the door.

Kylie sighed, trying to release the tension she felt at being alone with the Badon cousins, even if it was only for a short trip to the restaurant in the hotel, and tried to shore up her defenses as well. She was going to need every ounce of her control to keep those three men at arm's lengths. With each day that passed, it was getting harder and harder for her to try to remain apathetic in their presence. With one last glance at the mirror, she opened the door to Lachlan.

"Wow, you look so damn sexy, sugar." Lachlan perused her body and whistled through his teeth. "You'd better stick close to us tonight, Kylie, otherwise you are going to have every single man at the dinner vying for your attention."

"Yeah, right." Kylie stepped out into the hall when Lach stepped aside. "Let's go."

Kylie didn't wait for him, but hurried toward the front door. She paused mid-stride when she saw Xavier and Will waiting for them. All three men were wearing dress slacks and smart button-down shirts. Her body definitely liked what it saw, because her nipples pebbled and pussy clenched, releasing cream onto her panties. *Thank God I wore a padded bra. At least they won't be able to see how much they affect me.*

"You look good enough to eat, sweet thang." Will grinned and then winked at her.

Kylie met Xavier's gaze and although he didn't say anything about her appearance verbally, his eyes said everything. They ran the length of her body and back up again and when his gaze connected with hers, she could see the heat and hunger in it, but once again she chose to ignore it.

"We'd better go or we're going to be late." Kylie stepped toward the front door.

Xavier opened it and swept his arm out, indicating for her to take the lead. She headed toward their truck and had her hand on the back door when another hand covered hers.

"Allow me, sugar." Lach opened the door for her and then to her surprise, placed his hands on her waist and lifted her up into the truck. When her ass landed on the seat, she quickly scooted over to the other side of the vehicle and put on her seat belt. The three men talked about tonight's dinner and the wedding tomorrow, but Kylie was too tense to concentrate on what they were saying.

She had spent the day working on transcribing some medical texts and had been nearly finished when her e-mail alert had pinged. When she had opened the e-mail, hoping it was another batch of work, she'd had to cover her mouth to prevent a scream from escaping. Her eyes scanned the text.

Don't think you can escape me, bitch. I will find you and when I do, you know what will happen. Did you honestly think that leasing out your apartment and running would keep you safe? I warned what would happen if you went to the cops that night. Now you have to pay. Your time is running out, slut. Can you hear the clock ticking? Tick-tock. Tick-tock.

Kylie had started to call the police, but before she had dialed the first number, she had flung her cell phone aside. There was nothing the cops could do until this fucker came at her. Until then she was on her own. Or she would be as soon as Eva and her men left on their honeymoon. She wasn't about to spend the next three weeks in a house with three hot, sexy men. She was having enough trouble as it was not giving in to their caressing touches. Kylie was at breaking point in more ways than one. If one of them touched her one more time she was going to jump whoever it was and end up making a fool of herself.

Something Kylie had never thought she would do was end up caring for one man, let alone three. Slowly but surely, however, those three men had worked their way under her skin and she was in danger of caring for them more than she wanted to. There was only one thing left to do and that was get the hell out of their vicinity and quick, before she did something really stupid.

Kylie blinked when the truck slowed, and she realized that they were already at their destination. She had her seat belt off and the door open before the truck was turned off and then carefully stepped onto the side-step and down to the ground. The last thing she wanted right at this moment was to have one of them put their hands on her again. She was already going out of her mind with lust, and she didn't need that augmented any more than it already was. Turning back to the truck, she reached up and grabbed her purse and shawl from the seat and closed the truck door. As she stepped back, her body bumped into a warm, immovable wall. Large hands landed on her shoulders and she froze as her breath hitched in her throat.

"Next time wait for one of us to help you." Xavier's breath caressed her ear and she had a hard time controlling the shiver working its way up her spine and she could feel the heat emanating from his body.

Damn him. Damn them all. Why can't they leave me alone?

The heat left and she realized that Xavier had stepped back. Kylie turned around and headed toward the door to the hotel without once looking at him or Will or Lach as they came close. She pulled the door open with more force than necessary and quickened her step when one of them touched her lower back. When she inhaled, she knew it was Xavier who was close and hurried over to where Eva was seated between Quin and Pierson.

"Wow, you look hot, Kylie." Eva smiled and hugged her and Kylie kissed Eva's cheek before pulling away. "You are going to have to beat the single men off with a stick."

Kylie smiled and knew her smile didn't reach her eyes when Eva frowned at her.

"Are you okay?"

"Yeah, I'm good." Kylie smiled genuinely this time, glad that her friend had three men to love and take care of her and not wanting to put a damper on the night. She pushed her worries to the back of her mind, determined to get into the swing of the engagement party and enjoy herself for a change.

Kylie slid into the seat next to Gray, the last seat on that side of the long table, and then looked around at all the people. The number of men present far outweighed the women, but from what she could see, the women who were attending the evening were already hooked up. The blonde woman sitting across from her had a man on either side of her and both men touched her constantly. She looked up, caught Kylie watching, and smiled at her.

"Hi, I'm Tara Morten, and these are my husbands, Johnny and Clay."

"Hi, I'm Kylie."

"Ah, you're Eva's best friend."

"That would be me."

"Welcome to Slick Rock." Clay smiled and Johnny nodded his head as if agreeing with his brother's greeting.

"Thanks."

Throughout the night Kylie met the other ménage trios and quartets and hoped she could remember their names. Often when she looked up, she caught a few of the single men eying her, but she quickly looked away, not wanting to encourage any of them. She was aware of Xavier, Will, and Lachlan watching her constantly but chose to ignore them. Kylie had spent some time talking to three other new arrivals in town, cousins to the Morten brothers, Danny, Cain, and Bruce Morten. Bruce, who was known as Brutus because of his sheer size, was currently sitting to her right at the head of the table.

"How long have you been in Slick Rock, honey?"

"Just a few days," Kylie replied and didn't like the gleam in his eyes as they ran over the upper half of her body.

Kylie was beginning to feel the effects of being around so many people and picked up her glass of wine and took a big gulp. Her hand visibly shook as she placed the glass on the table and sweat popped out on her brow. Her breathing escalated and she was having trouble filling her lungs with air.

"Would you like to go out to dinner with me and my brothers one night?" Brutus asked.

"Um, no thanks. Excuse me." Kylie shoved her chair back and rushed toward the hallway to the ladies' room. She pushed the door open and sighed with relief when it shut behind her, closing out the noise.

"Oh my God," she sighed as she leaned on the sink. "I have to get out of here." Kylie tried to control her breathing. She inhaled to the count of five, exhaled slowly, and repeated the action a few times and was glad that the escalating panic attack had receded. Turning on the faucet, she splashed her hot face with cool water and then let it run over her wrists and hands. After turning off the water, she grabbed some paper towel and blotted her skin dry. She glanced up toward the door when it was pushed open.

"Are you okay, Kylie?" Eva asked as she moved further into the room.

"Yes, I'm fine."

"You don't look it. Were you having another panic attack?"

Kylie cursed under her breath. She had forgotten she had told Eva her reaction to being in a crowd, but she didn't want to upset her friend, so she outright lied. "No, I just got a little hot and bothered."

"Was Brutus harassing you?"

"No, he was just being polite," Kylie answered through clenched teeth. When she realized that Eva was watching her intently, she relaxed her jaw and tried to smile but knew she had failed when Eva frowned at her.

"You're as skittish as a cat on a hot tin roof. What the hell is going on?"

The fear that Kylie had been trying to keep at bay spiked and caused her skin to erupt in goose bumps, and a shudder wracked her body. Tears formed behind her eyes and she tried really hard to not let them fall, but Eva knew her too well. Eva rushed forward and wrapped her arms around her and hugged her tight.

"Tell me what's wrong, Kylie. I'm not leaving this bathroom until you do."

Kylie held in the sob forming in her throat and took a deep breath. She hadn't intended to tell Eva what was scaring her, but the words blurted from her mouth before her brain kicked into gear.

"I think he knows where I am."

"Fuck!" Eva drew back and Kylie laughed because Eva hardly ever swore. "Why do you think that?"

"I got an e-mail."

"What did it say?"

Kylie repeated the e-mail word for word, since it seemed to have embedded itself into her brain, and then wanted to curse as Eva paled.

"Wait here," Eva commanded and rushed out.

Kylie didn't want to face Eva's fiancés and their pity. She didn't want to face the Badon cousins either. She felt like her life was careening out of control and she was heading for a crash landing. The best thing she could do was leave. She was already headed toward the bathroom door, intending on leaving through the rear exit she had seen as she had walked toward the ladies' room, but before she had even placed her hand on the door handle, the door swung open. A very tall, dark-haired, muscular man entered the room with Eva and her men behind him. Eva stepped around him and introduced them.

"Kylie, this is Sheriff Luke Sun-Walker. My men have already told him about your trouble."

"Hi, Kylie, it's nice to meet you, but I'm sorry it's under such harrowing circumstances."

Kylie couldn't find her voice, so she nodded instead.

"I'd like to come over in the morning and take a look at that e-mail. Does nine o'clock suit you?"

"Yeah, that's fine." Kylie had barely finished answering the sheriff before the bathroom door burst open. She should have known that the Badon cousins would see something was going on.

"What the hell is this?" Xavier asked, pushing his way into the now-crowded ladies' room, and he didn't stop moving until he was standing at her side. Will and Lachlan came forward until she was surrounded by them. Xavier was on one side, Lachlan on the other, and Will squeezed in behind, between her and the bathroom wall. She took a step forward but Will wrapped his arms around her waist and pulled her back up against his front. Their scent enveloped her and the tension that had invaded her body began to dissipate. Kylie frowned over that occurrence. She felt safe and protected and she didn't want to move, aware now that she was surrounded by their heat and ensconced in Will's arms. But the last thing she needed and wanted was to be attracted to these three men. What if the asshole who had threatened her knew where she was? How would she feel if one of these men, or God forbid, Eva or one of the other women got hurt because of her? There was no way in hell Kylie was about to put anyone else in jeopardy

The walls to the room began closing in on her, and Kylie wanted nothing more than to escape. Sweat once more formed on her brow and upper lip and her breathing hastened. Her heart was pounding so hard and fast in her chest she looked down to see if the rapid beating was visible. Her legs began to tremble, as did the rest of her body, as adrenaline surged through her system. She pushed against the arms around her waist and was surprised but relieved when they released her. Her vision shimmered and everything wavered as she took one step and then another. She could see Eva and the men in front of her frowning, but she didn't want their pity. She locked onto the only thing familiar and stared at her best friend as she moved. Her body felt like it was walking through quicksand, her limbs heavy and even though she felt like she was moving rapidly, she somehow knew she wasn't. Kylie could see Eva's mouth moving, but because of the way her blood was rushing through her body, any other noise was drowned out. Just as she reached out to Eva, darkness began to close in. It was like looking through a tunnel with the walls moving closer and closer to her. Her sight diminished until she could see nothing at all and then she sighed as the darkness swamped her.

Chapter Six

Lach moved fast and caught Kylie before she could hit the ground. He gently swung her up into his arms and looked at the sheriff. "Call a doctor and get them here fast."

Luke was already on the phone and Quin, Gray, and Pierson rushed forward to help him.

"I've got her, but we need to get her someplace where she can lie down."

Gray held the door to the bathroom open and stepped back so he could get through. His brothers, Eva, and his cousins rushed through the dining room of the hotel to the foyer after him. Pierson hurried to the reception desk, explained the situation, and asked for a room key. The receptionist hesitated, but then sighed resignedly and handed the key to Pierson, who then led the way down another hall and opened the door to a hotel room.

Lachlan carefully placed Kylie onto the bed and, with his brothers' help, removed her shoes. He wanted to strip off her dress, but there was no way he was letting any other men besides his brothers see their woman half-naked. Xavier must have been thinking the same thing. His brother's next words proved him right.

"Why don't you leave Kylie to us? We'll make sure she's cared for. You have guests to see to."

Lachlan waited until just he and his brothers were left in the hotel room before he gently turned Kylie onto her side and drew the zipper down the back of her dress. With his brothers' help, they had removed her dress and then placed her under the covers. Just as they covered her up, a knock sounded at the door. Pierson opened it and let the doctor in.

"What seems to be the problem?"

Xavier explained about the threat to Kylie and then told the man she had just collapsed in the ladies' bathroom. Lach also told him what he had seen happening to their woman.

He and his brothers watched avidly while the doctor examined Kylie. He took her pulse and blood pressure and just as he was listening to her heart, she moaned and shifted on the bed and then opened her eyes. Lach sat on the side of the bed and placed his hand on her thigh, giving her a comforting caress.

"Don't panic, sugar. This is the doctor and he's checking you over."

"I don't need a doctor," Kylie snapped and then she glanced toward the medical practitioner sheepishly. "Sorry, but I'm fine."

"So you've had panic attacks before?" the doc asked.

"Once or twice."

"Mm, you need to get more rest, young lady. You are totally exhausted but I can understand why you'd have trouble sleeping."

"You told him?" Kylie asked accusingly.

"Now, now, don't get upset. I needed to know everything so I could treat you. Apart from being tired and underweight, you are healthy enough. You need to eat and rest more. If you continue to have trouble sleeping, come and see me in a week. I may have to prescribe some sleeping tablets."

Kylie nodded to the doctor and then thanked him for his time, but Lachlan could see the determination in her eyes to cope on her own. She was such a stubborn little thing and he and his brothers weren't about to let her get away.

The doctor left her his card on the bedside table, and once he'd left the hotel room, she glanced at all of them and pushed her chin out while clutching the covers. "Could y'all please leave so I can get dressed? Who the hell undressed me anyway?"

"We did, sweet thang," Will answered, his eyes on hers. "We were worried about you and wanted to make sure you were comfortable."

Lach watched as pink suffused her cheeks and then traveled down her neck and then she glanced away as if embarrassed. He reached over and gripped her chin, bringing her gaze up to meet his. "You have nothing to be embarrassed or ashamed about, sugar. Your body is perfect and so fucking sexy."

Kylie turned her head and dislodged his hand, but he saw her swallow and he could tell his brothers had heard the audible action as they both moved closer. Lach looked up when Xavier sat down on the bed close to her hip. She pulled back, but her pulse was beating rapidly in the base of her neck and her breathing was quicker than usual. He looked up into her green eyes and noticed that her pupils were dilated. As much as she tried to hide it, Kylie Mailing was turned on and not just by one of them. All three of them got to her and he'd had about as much as he could take. Obviously, so had Xavier.

Xavier palmed her cheeks between both his hands and then swooped in. His brother didn't start the kiss off slow and ease Kylie into it. He devoured her mouth like a starving man. Lach was just as hungry if not hungrier than his older brother to taste their woman. He gripped his aching cock and shifted it, trying to relieve the throbbing, but it didn't help. Then Kylie moaned and whimpered and reached up to grab at Xavier's hair.

Lachlan was done for.

Lachlan moved to the other side of Kylie and reclined beside her. His body temperature rose another several degrees when he saw the way her tongue danced with Xavier's. He wanted to taste her mouth, her throat, her breasts, her skin, her pussy, and everywhere in between. He was so damn hungry that he was shaking with it. Xavier slowed the kiss and finally eased away from her. Lach didn't give her a chance to move, he literally pounced on her. His body blanketed her, but he didn't put any of his weight on her and there was still a gap between his body and hers. He wanted nothing more than to rip the covers away as well as his clothes and her underwear and then have her naked body pinned beneath his, but he didn't want to scare her away. Instead of devouring her like Xavier had, he gently placed his lips against hers and brushed them back and forth.

Her breath puffed out from between her parted lips on a moan, and Lachlan slipped his tongue in between them and her teeth. He groaned as her sweet taste coated his taste buds and he wondered if the cream from her pussy would taste just as sweet. But first he wanted to savor her mouth with his. His tongue slid along hers and then he explored her inner cheeks and teeth before moving back to tangle with her tongue once again. She tasted so sweet and right, as if he was complete for the first time and had finally come home. Now all they had to do was convince her to take a chance on them and trust them. A not so gentle thump to his shoulder let him know that Will was just as eager to get a taste of their woman and wouldn't wait much longer. Lach lowered his body along hers, but didn't give her his full weight, and then he lifted his mouth from hers.

Kylie was so damn fucking beautiful with her lips vibrantly red and kiss swollen, her eyes glazed over with passion, and her cheeks tinged a pink hue. But underneath her arousal, she looked so damn lost and tired. There were dark smudges beneath her eyes, a testament to lack of sleep over a couple of weeks, and beneath that flush, her skin was a creamy white and she was so damn thin she looked fragile. He pushed up onto his knees and elbows and rolled over off to the side, giving Will room to move closer to her as he crawled onto the end of the bed.

The dazed look in Kylie's eyes changed to confusion and then anger took over. Will was reaching for her as he moved up between her splayed thighs, which were still covered by the blankets, but he halted when she held a hand up, palm facing out, and then she looked from him to Xavier and Will and then took a deep breath, ran her fingers into her hair as she pushed up into a sitting position and then glared at them.

"What the hell do you think you're doing?"

"If you have to ask us, baby, then we weren't doing a very good job," Xavier answered calmly.

"I can't do this."

"Why?" Will snapped out the question, surprising him and Xavier, and by the look on his face, himself.

"I can't have a relationship with one man, let alone three. It's not right. As far as I know, it's illegal, and I have enough to deal with without having to worry about anyone else."

"First off, having a relationship with more than one person is *not* illegal," Lachlan said firmly. "Is that what you think about Eva's relationship with our cousins?"

"No!" Kylie answered emphatically and then bit her lip when she realized what she'd done.

"Thank God for small mercies," Lach muttered, but the glare Kylie gave him told him she'd heard him. He gave a shrug of his shoulders.

"Secondly, if you would let us help you, if you would lean on us for a while, you wouldn't have to worry so much. We can protect you, Kylie." Xavier rose from the bed and began to pace the room.

Will got off the end of the bed and took a couple of steps away before turning back to pin her with his stare. "We could have something good between us if you would let us get close to you, sweetness." He held up his hand when Kylie opened her mouth, no doubt to refute Will's statement. "Don't you dare deny the attraction between us, honey. Do you think we don't see the way your body reacts to us when we're near you? Your nipples get so damn hard they try to push through your bra and top, and we can damn well smell the cream leaking from your pussy."

Another blush crept up her neck and cheeks and she looked down to the bed cover and began to trace the tip of her finger over a flower.

"What the hell are you so scared of, sugar?" Lachlan asked, deciding to put it out into the open. He and his brothers had already figured out she was scared and not just of the fucker out to get her. There was something else going on here, and he was determined to get to the bottom of it.

She lifted her head and thrust her chin out at him. "I'm not scared of anything."

"Prove it," Xavier bit out.

"I don't need to prove anything to anyone."

"No, you're right, you don't." Lachlan sighed and headed to where her dress was draped over a chair. He grabbed it, walked back to the bed, and handed it to her. "Why don't you get dressed and then we'll head on back to the house. I think you should be in bed. The doctor said you need to rest, and with the wedding tomorrow, I think you should call it a night."

"I'll wait out in the hall for you, sweet thang," Will said as he opened the door. "Xavier and Lachlan will let Eva and our cousins know we're leaving."

Lachlan headed toward the door as Xavier and Will exited the room but looked back at Kylie over his shoulder. "Are you sure you're okay, Kylie?"

She glanced off to the side before meeting his gaze again and said on a sigh, "I'm fine."

Lachlan stepped through the door, but before pulling it all the way closed pinned her with his stare once more. "Don't think whatever we have between us is over, honey. We know you want us just as much as we want you, and we *are* going to find out where this thing between us is going."

* * * *

Kylie stared at the closed door and wondered what the hell she had got herself into. First she had some crazy rapist after her, and now she had three men who wanted to have a relationship with her. Why did everything have to happen at once?

But then the little devil on her left shoulder whispered in her ear. Maybe Xavier, Will, and Lachlan didn't want to have a relationship at all and just wanted to use her for sex. There was no way in hell she was going to let them use her as a receptacle to relieve their sexual urges. Kylie thought back to how they had treated her over the last few days, that was, when she hadn't been hiding from them.

Xavier was the most serious of the three brothers. He was a straight down the line sort of man and didn't hesitate to call it how he saw it but she had seen the way he had been holding back when dealing with her. She wondered if that was because of all the stress she was under or if he was afraid she couldn't handle his straight-laced, hard-ass ways.

Will was the playful one. When he was around he was always trying to get her to smile but she could see underneath that playful exterior that he had great depths to his soul and kept his serious side hidden. Or maybe he was just waiting for her to get to know him better before revealing his true self. Then there was Lachlan or Lach as the others called him. Lach could be as hard as Xavier. She had seen it in his eyes tonight when he had declared that whatever was between them wasn't over. Determination had lit up his gaze from the inside and she knew that even if she found a place of her own that those three men weren't going to leave her alone.

And if she was honest with herself, Kylie had loved being around everyone in Eva's house. Of course, she had spent most of her life alone and lonely, except for the time she had spent with Eva, but she finally realized that she had made the choice to be by herself because of her claustrophobia. It wasn't until she was staying with her best friend and fiancés, as well as their cousins, that she realized just how damn lonely she been and how she had let her phobia force her into a life of solitude.

It had gotten so bad that whenever she had to leave her apartment she would begin to hyperventilate and sweat. Shopping was a nightmare for her with so many strange people around, so she had even begun to have her groceries delivered. She and Eva used to go out regularly, but when her mother had become ill, Kylie had spent her time taking care of her and stopped socializing. When Eva had moved away, Kylie had been devastated, but then she had been happy that her best friend had found the loves of her life. That's what Kylie wanted. She was sick and tired of living in her secure, comfortable little bubble and even though she was scared shitless about that evil man finding her, her fear of him had given her the push she needed to start living her life again instead of just existing.

Leasing out her apartment and leaving her safe environment had been one of the hardest things she had ever done in her life, but she had taken the first step and didn't intend to step backward now. Life was meant to be lived and enjoyed through good times and bad, and she wasn't about to let her anxieties stop her from taking the next step.

And that included finding out what those Badon cousins wanted from her. She decided right then that if they were just looking for sex, fine. She could do that. It might end in heartbreak, but she'd been through loss before and she could deal with it again. With a stalker hot on her heels, everything in her life felt uncertain. She had to start living in the now, even if that meant jumping in with both feet and hoping to God it didn't blow up in her face.

Chapter Seven

The moment Kylie stepped out of the hotel room, she felt like her whole life had changed. Lachlan was waiting for her, just like he said he would, and as soon as she was close enough, he placed his hand on her back and began to rub in soothing circles, as if he could feel the tension emanating off of her and her need to have some human contact. God, it had been so long since someone had just held her. The thought of leaning against Lachlan's firm, masculine body and having his arms wrapped around her sent a massive urge through her, and she had to concentrate on not throwing herself into his arms.

Lach didn't speak as he walked down the hallway beside her and she kept her eyes down so he wouldn't see the yearning she felt in her eyes. A noise ahead of her drew her attention and she lifted her head. Her gaze locked onto Xavier's and no matter how hard she tried, she couldn't look away. She felt as if she was drowning and falling into him. Her pussy clenched and gushed and her nipples pebbled into hard little buds. The material of her lace bra felt abrasive on her sensitive nipples as she took rapid shallow breaths, and as she watched, Xavier's eyes turned from cool to hot within a split second.

How she missed seeing him move was beyond her, but one moment she was walking toward him with their eyes locked and the next moment he was in front of her and scooping her off her feet. Kylie whimpered as the heat of his body seeped into her as he cradled her against his chest, and she slung an arm around his neck for stability as he hurried toward the exit.

"Will, hurry up and bring the truck out front. We need to get Kylie home, *now.*" Xavier looked down at her while he spoke to his brother, but his next words were for her. "We'll take care of you, baby. You won't regret it, I promise."

"Wha…" Kylie didn't get to finish her question because in the next moment Xavier's lips were on hers and she was lost. His tongue pushed into her mouth and curled around hers before withdrawing, pulling hers into his mouth. She moaned and mewled as he began to suck on her tongue. Her body flashed from simmering to boiling hot in a nanosecond, and she lifted her other arm up and threaded her fingers through his hair. A cool breeze wafted over her but it did nothing to cool the fire coursing through her body. Xavier released her tongue, swiped his across her bottom lip and then lifted his head. It was then that she realized they were outside and Lachlan had opened the back door to the truck and was holding it open as he stared at her.

She glanced toward Will and he, too, was looking at her as if he was starving. Kylie lowered her gaze and wondered how she had let things get so out of hand and in public, too. She shifted in Xavier's hold and tried to look over his shoulder into the hotel to see if anyone had seen the way she had behaved, but his hold tightened on her, drawing her attention.

"No one saw us, baby. Relax, the only people who will ever see your passion from now on are me and my brothers." Xavier got into the backseat of the truck, taking her with him, but he was careful as he passed the door and made sure that no part of her body hit on the frame of the truck.

Once on the backseat, he didn't relinquish his hold on her but placed her on his lap and hugged her tight. Kylie nuzzled her nose against the skin of his neck and inhaled deeply. She sighed with arousal and contentment as his unique, clean, manly scent filled her olfactory sense and knew she was in deep trouble. She'd never wanted to smell a man before, and the fact that she had just inhaled his scent had her mind on alert. But then the fear slid away when he threaded his fingers into her hair and gently tugged her head back.

She looked up at him through narrowed eyes and watched as he slowly lowered his head toward hers.

Is he giving me time to move away? Maybe he's waiting for me to say no. I can't do that. God, I want him so fucking much. I want them all so damn much I'm burning up.

It didn't seem to matter at the moment that they only wanted her for sex. Nothing mattered but extinguishing the burn running through her body. She'd never felt so out of control before, had never felt the heat running through her veins or the yearning to have them touching her and holding her.

No, that isn't true.

She had needed from the moment she had set eyes on them and she was about to find out if they could take care of every one of those needs. Kylie was so scared deep inside, scared that they meant more to her than they should, scared that her heart would shatter when they left, and scared that she would never be able to put the pieces back together again. But she was more scared of not knowing what it felt like to be loved by these three men.

She sighed into Xavier's mouth when his lips finally met hers. He brushed his lips back and forth, testing her response and she couldn't hold anything back. Not anymore. She'd wanted, needed this from the very first, and it was finally happening. Her heart thumped rapidly against her chest and her breath puffed out in a rush as Xavier deepened the kiss. His tongue pushed in between her lips and teeth and he explored every part of her mouth. She heard a moan and realized it had come from her and then she mewled with rapturous delight as his hand left her waist, smoothed up her side and cupped her breast.

Her nipple hardened and ached as he kneaded her fleshy globe, and she wanted to scream at him to touch her hard peak, but there was no way she was ending their hungry kiss just so she could speak, so she arched up into his touch, letting him know how much she wanted, needed.

The cry that left her mouth was muffled as he tangled his tongue with hers, but she heard his echoing moan, and shivers of arousal traversed her body as feminine power raced through her. She was giving him pleasure, too, and she wasn't even touching him yet. That was a heady feeling. Kylie gasped when his fingers scratched and tickled over her turgid peak. She thrust her hips up and placed her hands on his shirt, running them over his chest and torso.

God, he was so fucking muscular. He felt like hard stone covered with warm skin and she still hadn't touched his naked flesh. Without any conscious thought, her fingers undid buttons, pushed cotton aside, and then her hands were on his bare skin. The light dusting of hair on his chest was an aphrodisiac to her senses, but still she craved more. She wanted everything. Her hands raced down his torso to his stomach then to the waistband of his pants. She was grappling with his belt, trying to get inside, and nearly screamed with frustration when he ended the kiss and grasped her wrists in one hand.

She looked up into his lust-filled eyes and then held her breath as he skimmed a hand up her inner leg, from knee to thigh beneath her dress. Pinpricks of light formed before her eyes and she released the breath she had been holding and then gasped in more air. Her lids lowered when his big, warm hand brushed against the crotch of her panties. She cried out and arched her hips up when he placed a hand over her mound, covering her completely.

"You are so fucking passionate, baby. I can't wait to taste that delectable-smelling cream. I am going to make you come so hard and I'm going to drink down all your juices."

If he hadn't been holding her she would have been thrown from his lap when the truck swerved and then jerked back straight.

"Jesus, Xavier. I'm trying to fucking drive here. Stop that shit until we get home," Will yelled.

Kylie looked up and met his glittering gaze in the rearview mirror, and if he hadn't looked away, back to the road, she didn't think she would have been able to break the connection. Her eyes shifted to the seat next to Will and she met Lachlan's eyes. He was half turned in his seat and he was looking at her with such heat and hunger she wasn't sure why the heat from his gaze hadn't singed her skin.

"Lift her dress up, man. I want to see," Lach said in a raspy voice.

Goose bumps erupted over her skin and a shiver wracked her frame and she nearly screamed in frustration when Xavier removed his hand from her pussy. But then her breath hitched in her throat when he used both hands and lifted her dress up to her waist, baring her upper thighs and her lace-covered mound. Lach's eyes zeroed in on her pussy and he groaned loudly before lifting them to her face again.

"She is so fucking wet. I want to see her cunt. Take her panties off."

Kylie's chest rose and fell rapidly as she gasped in air, but not once did she look away from Lachlan's hungry stare. Not even when Xavier's fingers moved to her hips as he slid his thumbs beneath the elastic of her panties. He pushed them down as far as they could go while she was still sitting on his lap and then he wrapped an arm around her waist and lifted her ass up and, one-handed, pushed them down her legs, finally pulling them off over her shoes. His hand stayed down low and he shoved her high heels from her feet.

He pulled her back onto his lap, so she was now sitting with her ass snuggled up against his stomach and crotch, his long, hard cock pulsing against her back and the cheeks of her ass, with her legs hooked over either side of his as she faced Lachlan.

Xavier spread his legs wide, opening her legs as far as they would go and she felt heat suffuse her cheeks, feeling vulnerable at how fully exposed her pussy was. She moved her arms, intending to place her hands over her vagina to hide it from Lach's view, but Xavier thwarted her before she could cover herself. He grasped her wrists in his big, manly hands and brought them together, shackling them with one hand and lifting them up above her head.

"Clasp your hands together around the back of my neck, baby."

The authority and demand in his voice caused her pussy to clench, and more fluid leaked out.

"Fuck, our little honey likes being told what to do, bro," Lachlan gasped out, his voice sounding strangled. It was then that Kylie realized she had closed her eyes, and when she opened them, she saw that Lachlan's eyes were staring at her cunt. "She nearly came when you said that and I can see her cream dribbling down to her ass." Lachlan unclipped his seat belt and then with great difficulty he climbed through the center of the two front seats and into the backseat. "Turn around, Xavier."

Xavier turned so that his back was resting against the back door and she was facing Lachlan and the other door. Lach ran his hands up the inside of her thighs and then his fingers were caressing her pussy. She sobbed with pleasure at the teasing titillation of his light touch. He avoided her clit and her pussy hole, and she wanted to demand that he touch her. His hands lifted from her skin, but before she could voice a protest, he gripped one ankle and placed her foot up on the top of the backseat and then he placed the other on the headrest of the driver's seat.

"Keep your feet there, sugar. If you move, I will stop touching you." He looked at her expectantly and she gave him a nod. His lips quirked up at the edges in a slight smile and then he slid from the seat and landed on his knees on the floor, ducking under her upraised leg as he bent down until his head hovered over her pussy.

Kylie mewled at the first swipe of Lachlan's tongue through her wet folds and went to reach out to hold his head to her vagina, but Xavier gripped her forearms and placed them back behind his neck. Then Xavier's hands were on her breasts and he squeezed her nipples between thumb and finger, causing zings of pleasurable pain to shoot from her breasts straight down to her pussy, where Lach was still lapping up her cream.

His voice vibrated her folds when he spoke, enhancing the pleasure he was already giving her. "You taste so fucking amazing, sugar, so sweet and spicy. I am going to make sure I get a taste of this perfect little cunt every day."

Lachlan slid his tongue up her crevice and then his tongue flicked over her clit. She cried out as joy seared through her, but it still wasn't enough. She needed so much more. Kylie wanted him to fuck her, right here, right now.

"Please," she whimpered as he swiped her engorged bundle of nerves again.

"Please what, baby?" Xavier's voice rumbled over her as he pinched her nipples again.

"Please, fuck me."

"Not yet, sugar." Lachlan nibbled on her clit with his lips and teeth, and she arced up when he thrust a finger into her aching channel.

"Shit, yeah. Her pussy is so damn tight it's a struggle to get my finger inside her," Lachlan panted. "Relax for me, Kylie. I'll make you feel good, darlin'."

How the hell does he expect me to relax when my whole body is on fire?

"We're nearly home," Will said in a deep, gravelly voice. "Make her come now."

Lachlan withdrew his finger, and before she could protest, he was back with two. He slowly shunted his fingers in and out of her pussy as he licked and sucked her clit until he was inside her as far as he could go. Her internal walls rippled and grasped, clenching and releasing around those digits, trying to keep them inside her as he slowly withdrew. But he didn't withdraw totally, and when he pushed them back in, it was with greater speed. Her head rolled over Xavier's shoulder restlessly as bliss swamped her from all angles. And then he was shuttling his fingers in and out of her rapidly. Her womb became heavy and her juices leaked out continuously. Pressure built and built until she didn't think she could stand any more, and then Lachlan caged her clit gently between his teeth and flickered the tip of his tongue over her little pearl so fast she didn't stand a chance.

She pressed her head into Xavier's shoulder and screamed as nirvana hit. The spring inside her snapped, causing her vagina to clamp and release, clench and let go on the fingers still pressing in and out of her pussy.

"Yeah, that's it, baby, give Lach all that sweet cream," Xavier said into her ear, tweaking her nipples simultaneously, causing another wave of euphoric pleasure to wash over her.

When the last convulsion ebbed, she became aware of the four hands running over her body and the complete silence except for the heavy breathing of the four of them inside the truck.

Lachlan pulled her dress down so that it covered her sex. "You're a very sexy, passionate woman, Kylie."

"Let's get the hell inside," Will commanded, opening his door.

Lachlan got out and then held a hand out toward her. She placed her hand in his and would have fallen on her ass if he hadn't caught her. Her legs were weak after such pleasure and felt about as solid as water. He swept her up into his arms and then he was hurrying to the front door, which was already open.

Kylie looked back over Lach's shoulder to see Xavier following them, and when she glanced down his delectably muscular body, her eyes snagged at his protruding cock. From the looks of him, he wasn't lacking in any way in the penis department. She looked back to the front when Lach stopped moving and saw that they were in her room. He lowered her feet to the floor and Will stalked toward her like she was prey to his predator. Her recently satiated desire leapt and started to simmer once more.

He held her face between his hands, tilted her head to the side, and then slammed his mouth over hers. She mewled when he thrust his tongue in and tangled it with hers. He tasted so good she never wanted the kiss to end. More hands landed on her body and then the zipper to her dress was being lowered. Xavier and Lachlan made quick work divesting her from the rest of her clothes until she stood totally naked in front of three men. Will finally weaned his lips from hers, pinned her with his eyes, and then did a long, leisurely perusal of her naked form.

"You have the body of a goddess, sweet thang. I can't wait to get my cock buried into that sweet pussy." He lifted her into his arms and carried her toward the bed before lowering her onto the bottom sheet. She had no idea who had pulled the covers and top sheet back, and right at that moment she didn't care. Kylie had to concentrate really hard on not reaching for him when he straightened up and withdrew from her, but when he stepped back, she noticed for the first time that Xavier and Lachlan were completely naked.

Oh my God. They were masculine perfection and so damn confident. Both men stood off the side of the bed, arms folded over their chests, totally comfortable in their own skin. They were cut, their muscled definition enough to make any woman of any age drool, and they were all hers. At least for the moment. Xavier's cock was pointing straight at her. It was so big and heavy there was no way it would lie parallel to his body unless he was lying down. His penis had to be at least ten inches long, and if she placed her wrist next to it, it would be a struggle to see which was thicker. The head was a ruddy purple and there was a drop of fluid glistening in and on the slit.

Kylie absently licked her lips, which elicited a groan of male appreciation from both men. She looked over at Lachlan and bit the inside of her cheek to stop the moan that was forming in her throat from escaping. His cock wasn't as long as Xavier's but it looked to be bigger in circumference and she wasn't sure that she wanted his thick dick anywhere near her body. He must have seen her nervous trepidation, because when she lifted her eyes to his, he was frowning at her.

"Don't worry, sugar, I promise not to hurt you." He took a couple of steps forward and then cupped her chin. "I will fit inside your beautiful, slick pussy. You were made for us, baby."

"I—I don't think…"

A hot male chest connected with her naked back and she jumped at the unexpectedness of feeling another man's flesh brushing against hers. It felt so damn good she couldn't stop herself from moving from side to side, soaking up the contact of flesh on flesh. She hadn't forgotten that Will was in the room, but she had been so intent on studying the hot, hunky male forms in front of her that she'd sort of zoned out for a moment and hadn't felt when he had climbed onto the bed with her.

Will's hands ran up and down her side, causing her to shiver with anticipation and desire, but then he pressed a leg in between hers from behind and she had no choice but to spread her legs. Not that she would have pushed him away, because she was on fire and wanted them to put out her flames.

She was lying on her side and Will moved away and then rolled her onto her back. She looked up into his gray eyes and felt lost. He lowered his head to her and then he was kissing her. Oh God, it felt so good, she never wanted the kiss to end. The mattress dipped near her feet and on her other side and she knew Xavier and Lachlan had gotten onto the bed. Large, warm, callused hands ran up and down her shins and slowly traveled higher and higher. Another set of hands cupped her breasts and began kneading them and she cried out at the exquisite pleasure. The hands moving up the inside of her thighs gently pried her legs wide apart. If she hadn't been so turned on, she would have been embarrassed at being exposed, but she was aching with desire and wanted them to relieve that hunger.

A hot, wet tongue slid up through her dew-soaked folds and she cried out and thrust her hips up into that mouth, demanding more. She pulled her mouth from Will's and looked down her body and into Xavier's heated blue gaze. He winked at her, but his tongue never stopped moving on and in her pussy. He flicked the tip over her clit and when she mewled he did it again and again. The joyous sensations of having three men touching her, making love with her were almost too much to bear. She gasped when two mouths attached to her nipples and suckled her. Their mouths were unbelievably hot as they used their tongues to bestow pleasure on her. The internal muscles of her pussy clenched and pulsed as if begging to be filled.

When Xavier pushed a thick finger into her cunt, she opened her mouth to cry out, but all she could do was gasp soundlessly. Taking in another breath, she sobbed as pleasure assailed her. Xavier was now pumping his finger in and out of her pussy while laving her clit with his tongue. Tension charged through her like a speeding freight train and she realized the keening sound she could hear was coming from her. Electrical sparks zinged from her breasts where Will and Lachlan were still suckling strongly, and then her keening turned to a wail as bliss swept over her in great waves. The pressure that had been building within peaked and the inner coil snapped. Her cunt muscles clamped down on the two fingers still shuttling in and out of her pussy and cream gushed out of her vagina as she reached climax.

Never in her life had she felt such exquisite nirvana. The pleasure was so great it was excruciating, but it was also one of the most profound, poignant experiences of her life. The emptiness, which had been like a black hole in her heart, was gone, and in its wake was heart-wrenching emotion she had never thought to experience. Kylie's heart felt like it was overflowing with hope, love, and joy, and that was something she had never expected.

She wanted to be able to enjoy it, to lie in the bliss these three incredible men had given her, but it wasn't possible. After all the loss she'd suffered over the past few years, she ached to be cared for by these men. But until her stalker was caught, the more she cared about them the stronger her sense of dread became. She sighed and began to suspect that maybe a happy ending wasn't in her future.

Chapter Eight

Xavier had never seen a more beautiful sight in his life and he hoped to see it many more times. Kylie was such a passionate little thing and he wanted her in his bed and life forever. She was the most honestly responsive woman he had ever met and he couldn't wait to make love with her. He looked up to Will and Lachlan and could see the future in their eyes as they looked down at the gorgeous woman on the bed.

He gazed at Kylie's face as he ran his hands up and down her thighs, over her taut, concave belly, trying to bring her down slowly from her climactic high. Her eyelids fluttered open and he saw her green orbs were still glazed with the remnants of passion. As he shifted to his hands and knees, he realized he was shaking with lust, but as he looked at her stunning face he knew in his heart that what he felt for her wasn't just desire. It was love. He wanted to cuddle her close and tell her that everything would be all right, that he and his brothers would keep her safe. He wanted to tell her how he felt, how she had worked her way under his skin and into his heart for all time. But he knew she wasn't ready for such proclamations. He didn't want to push her away with words she wasn't ready to hear yet, so he kept his feelings to himself.

Her eyelids looked weighted as if she was having trouble keeping them open, and then she covered her mouth and yawned. As much as he wanted to make love with her right now, she needed sleep more. The dark smudges beneath her eyes were a testament to how exhausted she was, and even though his cock was screaming at him to plunge into her tight, wet pussy and connect with her on a physical as well as an emotional level, she needed to rest.

He laid his head on her belly and wrapped his arms around her hips. She felt so right in his arms and he wasn't about to let go anytime soon. He looked at Will and Lach and was pleased to see they were both worried about Kylie as well. They scooted down beside her so that she was nestled between them while he moved from between her legs and off the bed. He pulled the covers up and then pulled the quilt and top sheet out from the bottom of the mattress. There was no way in hell he wasn't sleeping in this bed with his woman. He got back on the bed and lay down across the foot then reached out and placed his hand on her leg.

"What are you doing?" Kylie asked around another yawn.

"Getting settled for the night," Will answered. "Close your eyes, sweet thang, you need to rest. You have a big day tomorrow with the wedding and all."

Kylie looked perplexed and Xavier had to hold in a chuckle. She had obviously expected him and his brothers to pounce on her after making her come. It was obvious that she'd never had anyone who would put her needs before their own. Well, their little darlin' was going to learn that her health and desires came first. It didn't matter that his dick was so hard it was jerking with each beat of his heart. It didn't matter that he would probably lie awake for hours on end with unrequited desire. Kylie was what mattered to him right now.

"Close your eyes, sugar." Lach moved in close and slung an arm over her waist and then he placed a gentle kiss against her temple. "Sleep, Kylie."

Her eyes slid closed and between one breath and the next, her breathing deepened and evened out. Their woman was asleep.

"She's going to continue fighting us," Will said in a low voice so he wouldn't disturb Kylie.

"Yes, she is," Xavier sighed.

"She can fight all she wants." Lachlan lifted his head to stare down at her. "She's gonna have to realize no matter what she does or says, she isn't going to push us away."

"She tries to act so tough and doesn't know we can see the fear and vulnerability in her eyes." Xavier rubbed his hand lightly over her leg.

"Did you see how scared she got after we made her come?" Lach asked.

"Yeah." Will nuzzled his nose into her neck and then looked over to Lach. "That about did me in. I wanted to pick her up, wrap around her, and hold her close, but she would have baulked."

"It's not just that asshole she's scared of. She's scared of how we make her feel. We're getting to her."

"So how are we going to handle this?" Will flopped back onto the pillow.

"We love her," Xavier said and hoped like hell that they could wear her down and get beneath those protective walls she had erected.

* * * *

Kylie had trouble containing her tears through the commitment ceremony. Eva had married Quin earlier that afternoon and now she stood in the backyard of their home beneath the rose-covered arbor while she recited her vows to all her men.

"Pierson, I love you so much. You are my love, my laughter, and my joy. I will spend the rest of my life by your side through the good times and bad. You are forever in my heart.

"Gray, I love you just as much. You mean more to me than words can say. You are the air I breathe and my light, and are also forever in my heart.

"Quin, I love you, too. You are my pillar of strength and even though I know we will butt heads often, you are forever in my heart."

The celebrant raised her hands and smiled at Eva and then looked up to the guests. "May you live and love long and enjoy the journey you are about to embark on."

Kylie wiped the moisture from her face as Pierson turned to Eva and drew her into his arms. He said something to her, but Kylie couldn't hear what. It had obviously been for Eva's ears alone. He kissed her and the crowd cheered and clapped as Eva was then kissed by her other two husbands. By the time they had finished, everyone was moving toward the large marquee where the reception would be held.

A hand landed on her shoulder and she looked up into Xavier's blue eyes. He placed a cloth into her hands and then rubbed her skin. "Are you okay, baby?"

"I'm fine, thanks." She looked at her hand to see a clean handkerchief and then used it to blot her eyes and face.

"You look so goddamn sexy in that dress, Kylie. You'd better stick close to us, or you're going to have the single men all over you."

Kylie didn't think anyone would be interested in her and rolled her eyes, but then she realized what he'd said and turned to face him.

"I'm serious," he continued. "I saw the way some of the guys are looking at you, looking at the skin you're showing in that dress. If you're not careful, they're going to be all over you."

"So? I'm a grown woman. I think I know how to handle flirty men."

His eyes narrowed. "Maybe you normally do, but this is different. These are Slick Rock men we're talking about here."

"And do you include yourself in these men I need to watch out for?" He opened his mouth to respond, but before he could, she held out a hand to silence him. "Listen, I don't need you or your Neanderthal brothers looking out for me. I can take care of myself." She whirled around and walked away.

The hair on the nape of her neck stood up on end, and although she wanted to look back over her shoulder, she didn't. She wasn't about to give Xavier the satisfaction of knowing she was aware of him, although after last night, she knew it was already too late. Just as she reached the tent, three very tall, muscular, bronze-skinned men moved into her path.

"Hi there, sweetie. I don't believe we've met. I'm Brent Eagle and these are my brothers, Jerome and Clifford."

"I'm Kylie Mailing, pleased to meet you." Kylie reached out to shake Brent's hand, but instead of shaking it, he just held it.

"We live in Mountain Village less than two hours from here," Clifford said.

"That's nice," she replied, not knowing what else to say.

"Are you a friend of the bride?" Jerome asked.

"Yes." Kylie snatched her hand back from Brent and stepped around them, feeling a little uncomfortable with the way they eyed her body. Cursing Eva mentally for picking a revealing dress that just screamed for attention, she hurried toward the bridal table and sat down next to Pierson. The three Eagle brothers were staring at her and she could see the interest in their eyes and that was the last thing she needed. She already had three men pursuing her. She didn't want or need any more.

By the end of the celebration, Kylie was exhausted. It had been such a beautiful day, but now all she wanted to do was have a hot shower and crawl into bed. Eva and her men had left for their honeymoon more than an hour ago, as had most of the guests. Felicity Eagle was currently helping Kylie transfer all the wedding gifts to the house while her husbands, Tom and Billy Eagle and Luke Sun-Walker, were talking to Tom and Billy's cousins as they folded up the tables and chairs and hauled them out to the clean horse float to be carted away.

After placing the last of the presents into the spare room next to the master bedroom, Kylie decided to take one more look around outside just to make sure nothing had been missed.

“I’m just going to check that we haven’t missed anything,” Kylie told Felicity.

“Okay, I just have a couple more cards and gifts to pair up and then we’re finished.”

Kylie nodded and then headed outside. It was nearly dark and with little light left she hurried to the pavilion. The Eagle men had moved out of sight and she had no idea where Xavier and his brothers were. She stepped into the tent and looked around, but everything had been cleaned away. All that was left was for the marquee to be pulled down, but that was a job for the Badon cousins that they would do tomorrow.

She pictured how happy Eva had been as she had shared her first meal with her husbands as Mrs. Badon. Her friend had glowed with love and happiness.

Kylie was so lost in her thoughts she didn’t realize that she was being watched, that something was terribly wrong, until it was too late to do anything about it.

Movement above her caught her attention, and she looked up just in time to glimpse the marquee falling toward her before her vision was completely obscured and she was smothered by the heavy fabric. As she struggled for air, a new panicked thought began to surface.

Do I smell smoke?

* * * *

The little cunt thought she could escape him. He almost laughed when he realized she’d run. She thought she was so smart, but he was much smarter. When he’d gone back to find out who she was, he’d also searched for her car. The apartment setup and the numbered parking garage had made his job easy. It had been easy as a snap of the fingers finding out who she was. The names of the apartment occupants were on the letterboxes in the foyer for anyone to see.

He'd spent a couple of years in the army and knew how to plan. He had learned to be patient and his patience would eventually pay off. He'd planted a tracker on her car so there wasn't any place she could run to. He would always find her.

He was staying in a cheap motel only a couple of hours from Slick Rock and had driven the distance every day, hoping for a glance of her. His persistence had paid off and now he was standing behind some bushes at the back of the property no more than a hundred yards away. The town had to be fucked up, because it looked like one woman was marrying three men. He glanced toward the bitch and imagined her beneath him as he pounded his cock into her cunt. She looked like she wanted it, wearing such a slutty green dress, which showed more than it covered, and he was just the man to show her what it felt like to be fucked by a real man.

As he crouched in the bushes, he imagined what he was going to do to her. It didn't matter that his muscles ached as he waited hours for his opportunity. He learned to watch for hours on end while serving in the military.

When the bride and grooms left and then guests also began to leave, he knew the time to move was almost at hand. There were still quite a few big men around, so he was going to have to be careful.

Then his chance presented itself and he ran toward the back of the large tent. The bitch was all alone and this was his break. Making sure to stay within the shadows, he skirted the tent, keeping an eye and ear out for the men who were nowhere in sight at the moment, and he released the ropes attached to the outside poles. When they were all loose, he pushed them over. He started near the entrance to the pavilion, cutting off her only avenue of escape, and then worked on both sides and finally the back. She yelled out as if pissed off when the canvas floated down around her, but he was so in the moment he didn't take any notice of what she said. Taking out his lighter, he sparked it to life and then placed the flame to the corner of the material.

He moved back into the shadows and back to the bushes and watched while the fire raced over the flammable cloth. Just as he was feeling triumphant that she couldn't escape, men came out running around to the backyard and began to douse the flames with water.

He cursed under his breath and crept to the road and hurried to his car. He took off without turning his lights on, not wanting to draw attention to himself. When he was a couple of streets away, he turned his headlights on and headed back to Mountain Village. He would have to be patient a little longer, but in the end, he would prevail. That cunt was going to die.

* * * *

Will and his brothers had just finished stacking the last of the folding tables into the horse float when he caught the stench of smoke in the air. Will passed the Eagle men on the ramp as they loaded up the last of the chairs.

"Is that smoke?" Lach asked as he sniffed.

"Yeah, we'd better investigate." Will hurried around the side of the house and into the backyard.

"What the fuck?" Xavier bumped his side as they both began to run toward the pavilion, which was now on the ground as fire licked across the canvas.

Lachlan yelled to the other men for help at the same time a familiar scream rent the air. Will ran the last few steps to the fallen tent and saw where Kylie was trying to frantically escape from beneath the heavy material. He didn't stop to think, he just reacted. Thank God he was always prepared. Will retrieved the knife he had sheathed and strapped at his ankle and leapt over the flames.

"Kylie, don't move, darlin'. I'll get you out." The squirming bundle stopped moving and he grabbed the material and began slicing close to her and then he grasped the cut and wrenched with all his strength.

Kylie's head appeared first and even though her face was covered in dirt and streaked with tears, he had never seen a more beautiful sight. He threw his knife off to the side and reached for her. His hands wrapped around her upper arms and he hauled her to her feet. She swayed a little so he scooped her up and then looked around to see where the fire was. There was no way he was letting his woman get burned. He sighed with relief when he saw the Eagle brothers were already dousing the flames. Will carefully carried Kylie over the smoldering material toward his brothers. Xavier reached out and clasped one hand while Lachlan grasped the other.

"Are you okay, sugar?" Lachlan caressed her cheek gently with the tips of his fingers.

"Are you hurt anywhere, baby?" Xavier lifted her hand to his mouth and kissed it.

Kylie coughed and then gasped out, "I'm fine."

"You don't sound fine." Will turned toward the house. "Let's get you inside so we can make sure you're not burned anywhere."

"I'll be in in a moment," Xavier called out as he headed toward Sheriff Luke Sun-Walker and Felicity's other husbands. "I want to know how that fire started."

"Did you see anyone around, Kylie?" Will asked as he carried her up the back steps to the porch. Lachlan was already holding the door open.

"No," she answered in a smoke-husky voice.

"Why don't you take her into the bathroom and get her into the shower?" Lach suggested. "I'll bring her something to drink."

Right now Kylie seemed too exhausted to argue with any of them. It had been a wonderfully emotional day but had turned frightening, and since she hadn't slept properly in weeks, Will could see it was all catching up with her. She rested her head on his shoulder and gave a sigh that sounded content. That little sound gave him hope. If she felt safe and cared for in his arms, didn't that mean she trusted him with her body if not with her heart?

Will sat Kylie on the counter and then turned away to start the shower. When he turned back, she had her arms around her body defensively and gave a little shiver.

"Come on, sweet thang, let me help you." He gripped her waist and lowered her to her feet and then helped her out of her dress. Once she was naked, he held her hand so she wouldn't slip while she stepped into the shower. He watched her standing under the warm water as he removed his clothes and then he got in with her. She was leaning against the tile wall as if she didn't have the energy to stand upright. Without saying anything, he reached for the shampoo and began to wash her hair. By the time he'd finished helping her clean up, some of the exhaustion had left her face and she was standing on her own.

Lachlan was waiting for her with towel in hand when he shut the water off. Will handed her off to his brother and reached for another towel. Lach wrapped Kylie in a large bath sheet and handed her a big glass of juice. She drank it quickly and when she thanked him, Will was pleased that some of the hoarseness had gone from her voice.

The door to the bathroom slammed open and Xavier stood in the doorway, his eyes searching out Kylie. He seemed to relax when he saw that she was safe and sound. "Did she get hurt?"

"No, the only damage was a bit of smoke inhalation and a sore throat." Will tied the towel around his hips.

"Luke and the others found footprints leading to the road. Whoever let that tent down and lit it up must have had a car waiting. Someone deliberately tried to hurt Kylie." Xavier sounded angry and Kylie looked worried.

"Xavier isn't mad at you, Kylie. He's worried for your safety just like Lach and I are."

Kylie's shoulders sagged. "See, I knew this would happen if I stayed here. An innocent person is going to get hurt and all because of me. I should just leave."

"No," Will and his brothers answered at the same time before continuing to talk amongst themselves.

"The rest of the town is on alert," Will said. "If any strangers show up, we'll know about it right away."

Xavier walked further into the bathroom and got out another clean towel and began to dry Kylie's hair. Will noticed that she looked a little pissed and was about to ask her what was wrong, but she beat him to it.

"I would appreciate it if you wouldn't talk about me as if I wasn't here."

Xavier's eyes narrowed and Will wondered how long before he and Kylie went head to head. He had been surprised by how much his arrogant, dominating brother had been holding back with their woman and wondered when he was going to step up to the plate. If Will had to guess—and because he knew his brother so well, guessing wasn't necessary—sparks were about to fly.

"What was your reply when I asked if you were hurt?"

"I told you that I was fine."

"Yes, you did. Why do you have to lie to us, Kylie? Why can't you ever answer truthfully?"

"I did," Kylie yelled. "God, you are such an arrogant asshole. I didn't get hurt. Okay, I breathed in a bit of smoke and have a slightly sore throat, but I wasn't injured for God's sake."

"What about the bruise and bump near your temple?" Xavier asked in a cool voice. "How did that happen?"

"Huh?" Kylie reached up and touched her head.

When her fingers connected with her wound, Will saw the slight tension in her mouth, refuting her claim that she wasn't hurt.

"That happened when one of the tent poles hit me on the head. It's nothing."

"When are you going to get it through that pretty little head of yours that we care about what happens to you? We care about you,

Kylie. When are you going to stop pushing everyone away?" Xavier nudged her chin up and studied the knot on her head.

Way to go, bro. Why not really scare her off and tell her we all love her?

Will watched Kylie's eyelids flutter closed. He wondered if she thought that having her eyes closed and not having to look at them would help to shore up her defenses again. He'd seen the shock in her eyes when Xavier had told her that they cared for her. But then he saw moisture trickle out from the corner of her eyes. Seeing her cry pulled at his heart strings, and before he thought about what he was doing, he nudged his brothers away and pulled her into his arms. Her arms crept around his waist and she clung tight to him as if he was her anchor in the middle of a raging storm.

He made shushing sounds and rocked her slightly while looking at his concerned brothers.

"What's going on, Kylie, love? Why are you crying?"

"I can't do this anymore. I just can't."

Xavier moved in behind her and wrapped his arms around her waist. Lachlan moved into her side and kissed her bared shoulder and then stroked her skin.

"What can't you do anymore, baby?" Xavier asked and placed a kiss on the top of her head.

"I can't fight this anymore. I've tried so damn hard, but no matter what I do, nothing works."

Will's knees nearly sagged with relief, but he needed to hear the words from her mouth before he and his brothers took this any further.

"What have you been fighting, sugar?"

Kylie inhaled deeply and then released it slowly before looking into his eyes. "I don't know where this chemistry between us is going or how long it will last. I tried to steer clear of you all because I don't want anyone getting caught up in my problems and inadvertently getting hurt because of association to me, but I want to be with you all."

"Sweetheart, you have to stop worrying about everyone else and start looking out for you. You care so much for everyone but you ignore the most important person and that is you. We can look after ourselves, Kylie. We're professionally trained bodyguards. You have to start trusting that we will do *anything* to keep you safe." Will bent down and placed an arm beneath her knees and the other around her shoulders and lifted her into his arms and headed into the bedroom. Lach and Xavier were right behind him.

"I know it takes a lot for you to trust, baby," Xavier said as Will lowered her to her feet. "Thank you for giving us a chance. I promise you that we will never do anything to hurt you on purpose."

Lachlan gripped her towel-covered hips and pulled her back flush to his front. "We are going to show you how we feel for you, sugar. By the time we're finished with you, there won't be any doubt in that hard head of yours."

Will bent down and kissed her with all the pent-up need and desire coursing through his body. He couldn't wait to try out all the steamy ways to express how much he and his brothers loved her.

Chapter Nine

Kylie hoped like hell she wasn't making the biggest mistake of her life. She was tired of fighting her feelings for these three men and keeping them at arm's length but she was also scared she would get her heart broken. Being trapped under that canvas tent had frightened her badly and she had decided that she was going to make love with the three Badon cousins. She had no idea what tomorrow would bring and she was going to grab hold of life and stop being so scared. Of course she was still frightened that her stalker would catch up with her but if he found her and ended up killing her she wasn't going to die with any regrets.

Will leaned down and kissed her and the thoughts that had been running around in her mind faded away. He gathered her in close and she melted into him as his tongue danced with hers. She mewled as his masculine flavor assailed her senses but she needed so much more. Will weaned his lips from hers and then moved aside for Lachlan. He didn't waste any time and took her mouth with a rapacious hunger.

Xavier was still behind her and he removed the towel from around her body. Goose bumps erupted over her skin as the cool air caressed her heated flesh. She shivered when Xavier ran his hands over her back, down to her ass. He squeezed her butt cheeks and then caressed his way up her sides until he was cupping her breasts, as if he was weighing them in his hands. Then he enclosed her fleshy globes in his big palms and kneaded them gently. A leg pressed in between hers from behind and she widened her stance.

Large, warm hands ran up and down the inside of her thighs and her pussy clenched with need and anticipation. Cream leaked from her cunt and she gasped for air when Lachlan ended the kiss. Hot air caressed her slit and she looked down to see Xavier's head between her legs. And then his mouth was on her cunt. Kylie simultaneously cried out and reached out so she wouldn't fall. If Lach hadn't held her shoulders and Xavier hadn't gripped her hips, she would have fallen into a melted puddle at their feet. She groaned as his tongue licked through her folds and lapped at her juices, and she couldn't help but thrust her hips, trying to get more friction on her engorged, aching clit.

"You are so fucking sexy, sugar," Lach rasped just before his hot mouth sucked a nipple into its depths. The tug of his mouth on her turgid peak along with Xavier's lips and tongue on her pussy had her right on the edge. Just as she thought she was about to go over the edge, they stopped.

She gasped. "W–Why…why did you stop?"

Xavier maneuvered from between her legs and then stood up behind her. "The next time you come, baby, I am going to be balls-deep inside that hot, wet pussy."

Xavier scooped her off her feet and carried her over to the bed. He placed her in the center of the mattress and followed her down. He took her mouth with hunger and then he kissed his way down her neck to her breasts. He sucked one nipple until she was crying out with need and then worked his way to the other. When he had her writhing and begging beneath him, he pushed up to his knees. Will and Lach had crawled on the bed on either side of her and took immediate advantage by bending over her and suckling at her breasts. Xavier nudged his brothers aside as he covered her body with his and kissed her again. He couldn't get enough of her. He seemed surprised but pleased that she hadn't baulked when his mouth touched hers. He had looked a little worried she wouldn't want to kiss him after he had eaten out her pussy, but she had no qualms. In fact she was the one who deepened the kiss, her excitement jumping up another level when she tasted her juices and his mouth. She drank him in as their tongues danced together.

She opened her eyes just in time to see Will tap on Xavier's shoulder, and he opened his eyes, but he didn't stop kissing her. Will held up a condom and Xavier took the open packet, removed it from the wrapper and rolled it down over his cock. When his hand brushed over her mound, she mewled into his mouth and arched her hips up. The silent demand she gave him seemed to spur him on even more, and from the look of determination on his face, he had no intention of ignoring it. He slipped his hands beneath the cheeks of her ass and gripped her flesh and then moved slightly, until his penis found her entrance and he began to enter her.

Xavier took his time as he rocked back and forth, gaining depth in small increments because she was so tight and he was such a big man. Her heart gave a hitch and filled with emotion, knowing that he was taking it easy with her as if he was scared of hurting her if he went too fast.

Kylie tilted her head back, breaking the kiss, and brought her hands up to clutch at his shoulders. "Oh my God. Oh my God."

She could feel his eyes on her, but the pleasure was so great she had her head tipped back and her eyes were squeezed tightly closed.

"Are you all right, baby? Am I hurting you? Do you want me to stop?" His concern for her filled her heart even more and she felt tears prick the back of her eyes. Once she had her emotions under control again, she looked up at him. His jaw was clenched tight and he had an almost tortured expression on his face. Sweat beaded on his forehead, a testament to the tight rein he had on himself.

"No. I've never felt…You feel so…You're stretching me and it feels so damn good."

"Baby, you feel like fucking heaven. You are so hot and wet." Xavier pushed in another couple of inches and held still again. She'd never experienced such sweet, overwhelming ecstasy before and she hoped like hell he felt the same way.

But she wanted more. She needed to feel him stroking in and out of her but most importantly she needed to feel connected to him on an emotional level. She reached up, wrapped her arms around his neck and pulled him down so that she was enveloped by his big body. “I’m not a delicate little flower. Hurry up and fuck me.”

Xavier’s control snapped and he shoved forward until he was balls-deep inside her. He withdrew and then surged back in. Her pussy rippled around his big cock, trying to hold him inside, and then he drew almost all the way out again. He set up a slow, easy rhythm at first and with each thrust of his hips he increased the speed of his pumping hips.

Kylie was frantic with carnal need and she sobbed as she clutched at his hair. Never had anything felt so right and so good. She felt feminine and sexy for the first time in her life and it was a heady experience. But more than anything she felt like she was home.

Xavier’s panting breaths puffed against her neck and then she mewled when he scraped his teeth along the side of her neck. He drove into her faster and faster and the tension that had been slowly building hovered right on the very edge of breaking.

He slid a hand beneath her ass and worked a finger in between her cheeks.

“I’m so close, baby. I want you to come on my cock,” he rasped against her ear.

Xavier’s finger applied pressure to her anus and that was all it took. Her insides lit up and she screamed as she hurtled over the edge into bliss. Wave upon wave of ecstasy washed over her. Her toes tingled and curled, her legs shook and her pussy clamped down and released. The contractions were so intense she saw stars and her body convulsed beneath his as she rode out the storm of rapture.

Xavier thrust into her twice more and then he growled low in his throat right before he, too, reached his peak. His cock pulsed and jerked inside her, enhancing her orgasm, and she moaned again. She felt the heat of his semen as it hit the little pouch at the end of the condom, causing another aftershock to ripple through her pussy. When the last ripples waned, she became aware of the silence in the room except for the heavy breathing from the four of them.

Xavier lifted his head and looked down into her eyes, and what she saw there had her breath hitching in her throat. He looked like he was in awe and she could see love shining out at her. “That was amazing, baby. It’s never been that good for me before. You are one beautiful, sexy woman. I could spend the rest of my life buried in this hot little pussy.”

Kylie didn’t know what to say to that, so she didn’t say anything, but her heart filled with joy at his words. Maybe he did really care for her after all. Instead of replying, she reached up and placed a kiss on his lips. Xavier took over the kiss but instead of devouring her he kissed her with such wonder it brought tears to her eyes. He sat up, slowly withdrawing his softening cock from her body, gave her a lingering look, and then headed into the bathroom.

Will’s voice drew her attention “That was amazing, sweet thang. How do you feel, Kylie? Are you sore?”

“No,” she said breathily. “I feel wonderful.”

“Are you ready for more, sugar?” Lach asked as he ran a hand up and down her side until he caressed the underside of one breast.

Kylie arched up into his touch. She’d never realized how sensitive that particular spot on her body was until now.

“Oh, I think you just found a sweet spot, bro.” Will smiled and then he, too, began caressing her in the same spot on her other breast.

Kylie moaned and she moved her legs restlessly as her libido began to surge again.

“Stop.” Kylie paused to gasp for breath and mentally cursed when they removed their hands from her and looked worried. “No, don’t stop. Don’t tease me, touch me.”

Will leaned down and captured her cry of pleasure as Lachlan began to suck on her nipple. She couldn't believe she was so turned on again after just having the most explosive orgasm of her life.

They both released her at the same time and she wondered if she had done something wrong, but then Will gripped her waist and flipped her over.

"Get onto your hands and knees, baby," he demanded in a deep, gravelly voice.

Kylie did as he asked and then Lach scooted up to the top of the bed. He moved so that he was resting his back against the headboard, his legs were between her arms and beneath her body and then he spread them wide. She didn't have to be told what he wanted. His position made it obvious. Kylie was so hungry. She fisted his cock and pumped her hand up and down his hard shaft a few times, eliciting a groan from him. A drop of clear fluid pearled in the slit at the top of his cock and she licked her lips. Then she lowered her head and swirled her tongue around the mushroom-shaped cap. Lachlan's gasp was music to her ears and she opened her mouth wide and sucked him in.

"Fuck yeah, sugar. Your mouth is amazing, so fucking perfect."

Kylie began bobbing her head up and down his cock and pumping her hand around the base at the same time. She was so intent on giving Lach pleasure, she was only vaguely aware of the mattress dipping behind her, between her spread legs. She inhaled through her nose and his musky scent embedded into her olfactory sense and ramped up her desire another notch.

Lachlan threaded his fingers into her hair and gripped it tight against her skull. He wasn't hurting her, but the sting to her scalp enhanced her arousal even more. She moaned when fingers slid through her slit, gathering her cream and then lightly caressed over her clit.

"Your pussy is dripping, sugar," Will rasped from behind her. "I can't wait to sink my cock into this pretty little cunt."

Kylie hummed her approval and Lachlan groaned. “Shit, Kylie, do that again. The vibrations from your voice feel like fucking heaven.”

Kylie hummed again and then mewled when the tip of Will’s condom-covered cock slid through her wet folds and the head of his dick was inside her. And then he was pushing into her. Kylie pushed back against him, trying to get him to go faster, which earned her a slap on the ass. Her butt cheek tingled and the heat from the slap spread. She sobbed with pleasure and her pussy clamped down on his cock.

“You liked that, didn’t you, sugar? You like a bite of pain with your pleasure,” Will said through panting breaths.

Lach tugged on her hair and tried to withdraw his hips. “Ease up, Kylie, or this will be over too soon.”

Kylie didn’t want to ease up. She wanted it all from him. After having a taste of his juices, she wanted more. She gripped his cock tighter and then bobbed up and down at a faster pace. Lach’s hand clenched in her hair and he tugged slightly. “Slow down, sweetie. I want us to come at the same time.”

She moaned her approval and slowed down, but when the tip of his cock was just inside her mouth she laved the underside, trying to enhance his pleasure, and made sure to stroke along the length of the large vein.

Will leaned over her and began to slide into her and retreat. Kylie could feel more of her cream spilling over his cock as he slowly forged his way inside her. The friction of his hard shaft caressing the walls of her pussy was pure bliss, but she still needed more. She wiggled her ass, trying to get him to push all the way inside, but he moved his hands and gripped her hips, preventing her from taking over control.

“We are in control in the bedroom, not you.” Will slapped her ass again.

We’ll see about that.

Kylie clenched her muscles and earned a groan from Will. She was so pleased with the response that she did it again and again, all the while giving Lach head.

"Kylie, I want to fuck your mouth, sugar," he panted. "Open your mouth for me, darlin'. I promise not to choke you."

Kylie removed her hand from his cock and opened her mouth into a wide *O*. Lach wrapped his hand around the base of his penis and then began to fuck her mouth. Now that she wasn't concentrating on giving him pleasure, she was able to let go and feel.

Will surged into her from behind. In this position, he was able to go so much deeper and her pussy felt even tighter than before. He increased the speed of his thrusts until his thighs and lower abs were making slapping sounds as they connected with her body while his balls tapped against her clit.

"You look so sexy with a cock in your pussy and another in your mouth," Xavier whispered against her ear. She slid her eyes sideways and met his heated blue gaze. Kylie had been so intent on making love with Lach and Will she hadn't realized Xavier was back from the bathroom.

"Her mouth is amazing," Lachlan gasped.

"Fuck me, I'm close," Will rasped and shifted behind her. He began to give her shallow strokes and she cried out around Lachlan's cock, making him moan. "Help send her over."

Xavier leaned underneath her and latched onto a nipple and then slid his hand down her belly. His finger tapped against her clit a couple of times and then he gently squeezed her sensitive pearl. That was it for her.

The coil that had been gathering in got tighter and tighter and her womb felt so heavy it was aching. Warmth spread from her uterus down to her sheath and down her legs. The muscles in her limbs were so taut she was shaking.

"Oh Jesus, so fucking good." Lach moaned.

Xavier pinched her clit and Kylie screamed around the cock in her mouth. Ecstasy grabbed hold of her and if Will hadn't been holding onto her hips, she thought she may just have hurtled up to the ceiling. Pleasure assailed her, her pussy grasped and released, clamped and let go, rippling around the cock still stroking in and out of her cunt. Her body quivered and quavered and then Will gave a mighty roar. His cock expanded and jerked as he spilled his load into the end of the condom.

"I'm coming, sugar, swallow me." Lach groaned as he pushed into her mouth.

Kylie took him in as far as she could and she tasted his sweet, salty essence on her tongue and relished every drop. She'd never wanted to suck any man off before. That was until she met the three Badon cousins. She released Lachlan's cock, gave the head a final lick, and was pleased at his groan. Kylie wanted to stay with them and be their woman, but she was afraid of putting them in danger. They had worked their way into her heart slowly but surely and she wondered what to do about it.

Chapter Ten

Kylie woke surrounded by heat. She stretched languorously, and froze when she bumped into a big, warm body and remembered that she had shared her bed with three men. She blinked a few times to dispel the sleep haze from her vision and then turned her head. Will had his head resting on his hand and he was watching her.

"Morning, sugar, how are you feeling?"

"Good."

"Are you sore, baby?"

Kylie lifted her head off the pillow and looked down the length of her body to where Xavier was lying across the bottom of the bed. "A little. I used muscles I didn't know existed last night."

"Why don't I help you in the shower, sweet thang?" Will asked from where he lay by her side. "Xavier and Lach can get breakfast ready, and after we've eaten we can head on out."

"Where are we going?" Kylie asked.

"We want your opinion on something, but for now let's go and get cleaned up." Will leaned forward and kissed her on the lips then he got out of bed. He had a wicked smile and gleam in his eyes and she wondered what he was up to. She knew a moment later when he flung the covers off of her and picked her up.

Kylie wrapped her arms around his neck and nuzzled him with her nose as he carried her to the bathroom. He slowly lowered her to her feet and she gasped as her body slid over his. She couldn't help but notice he had a hard-on. Will pulled the shower door open and turned the water on, and Kylie decided to play a little. She reached out and gripped his cock, pumping her hand up and down the length a few times.

He turned his heated gaze to her. “You’re playing with fire, little girl.”

“Oh yeah? Well, maybe I wanna get burned.”

Will spun around and grasped her waist and carried her into the shower. She giggled, feeling lighthearted for the first time in weeks, and then spluttered as he’d placed her under the water flow and she ended up with a mouthful of water.

“Shit, sorry, Kylie. Are you okay?”

Once she finished coughing she turned to him and smiled and watched as his frown changed to a cheeky grin. “I love it when you laugh, sweetheart. You should do it more often.”

“I guess I haven’t had much to laugh over lately.”

“No, I suppose not, but if we have our way, you’ll be laughing all the time.”

Kylie fell a little more in love with him then and there. She wanted to tell him how she felt, but until the asshole stalking her was caught, she was going to keep her feelings close to her chest. It may have been a convoluted way to think, but if she didn’t tell Will and his brothers that she was falling in love with them, then, if something happened to her, hopefully they wouldn’t be hurt.

Will grabbed the bottle of shampoo and poured some into his hand and began to wash her hair. After she rinsed the suds out, he massaged in some conditioner and then washed her body with shower gel. By the time she was clean and the conditioner had been rinsed off, she was hot with need. He quickly washed himself and then let the water wash the soap bubbles away but kept his eyes on her as she shifted from foot to foot, restless with desire.

“Lean back against the tile, Kylie.” Will gave her a hungry look. When she’d done as he told her, Will knelt down and tapped her thighs. “Spread those legs for me, honey.”

Kylie parted her legs and then watched with hungry fascination as he hunched down and licked her pussy. She cried out when he slid his tongue through her petals and sucked her clit into his mouth. The tip of a finger pushed into her cunt and then he scraped his teeth over her clit. The orgasm hit her hard and fast. Her breath caught in her throat on a soundless cry as rapture swept over her. Will wrapped an arm around her hips when her legs threatened to give out and used his free hand to caress her soothingly as she came back down. When she was once more steady on her feet, he stood up, gave her another quick rinse, and turned the water off.

"What about you?" she asked.

"I'm fine, sweet thang. I love to see you come apart for me. Come on, let's finish up and get some breakfast. I'm starving."

She fell even harder for him because he had just proven to her that he wasn't in this relationship just for sexual gratification. The words were on the tip of her tongue, but she held them back.

Lachlan and Xavier were just placing the food on the table when she and Will entered the kitchen. The smell of bacon, eggs, and toast made her stomach growl. "Sit down, baby. I'll just get your coffee." Xavier brought her coffee over and they were quiet as they ate their breakfast.

Kylie helped clean up the mess and after brushing her teeth was ready to go. Lachlan helped her into the backseat of the truck and then got in with her. Will and Xavier were in the front.

"Where are we going?"

Xavier glanced at her in the rearview mirror. "We've been looking for a ranch to buy and may have found the perfect place, but I would like your opinion on the house. A female can see things that men can't. We'd really appreciate your judgment on whether you think the place is worthwhile."

"Okay, I'd love to help." She smiled. "Thanks for trusting me."

* * * *

Xavier couldn't get over the change in Kylie since he and his brothers had made love with her last night. She looked so much lighter and happier, as if the weight of the world had lifted off of her shoulders. If he had his way, she would look like that from now on. Although he really did want her view on the house it wasn't because he needed any help. He wanted her to like it as much as he and his brothers did. He, Lach, and Will had already seen the place once before. It had everything needed for a viable ranch with all the outbuildings and fencing. The house was big and in good repair. It was long, two stories, plenty big enough for a wife, three husbands and a family. All it needed was a coat of paint inside and out and for the kitchen to be updated. And since they wanted Kylie in their lives forever, her viewpoint on the house mattered.

The ranch was on the outskirts of Slick Rock, and fifteen minutes later he was pulling into the driveway. He drove slowly so that Kylie could look around at everything. He stopped in front of the long two-story ranch house and turned off the ignition.

"Oh my, it's beautiful," she whispered as she got out of the truck.

Xavier got out and clasped her hand and led her up the steps of the wrap-around porch and to the front door. He withdrew the key and pushed the door open.

The hardwood floors gleamed in the sunlight streaming through the windows, and he pulled Kylie further into the house. There was a short hallway that opened up into a large living room that could hold two sofa settings.

Xavier didn't say anything, just watched as expressions flit across her face as she explored. He glanced back at his brothers, who were following close behind and saw they were watching Kylie just as avidly as he. There were six bedrooms. The master bedroom was huge and so was the en suite. There were two other bathrooms and a study downstairs.

"The house is amazing. All it needs is an updated kitchen and some paint."

"That's what I thought, too. I'm glad we're on the same page." Xavier guided her toward the front door. "Do you want to see the barn and look around outside?"

"Yes," Kylie answered, and he felt hopeful when he heard the excitement in her voice.

After spending three hours exploring, Xavier went and locked up and they all got back into the truck and headed toward town. It was close to lunchtime and he was hungry. He decided that eating at the diner was a good idea.

"What did you think, sugar?" Lachlan asked.

"I think it's perfect. Everything has been maintained and there isn't much work needed to get the house up to scratch. If I were you, I would put an offer in."

"That's what we thought. I'll call the estate agent this afternoon. Now let's go get some lunch."

After having lunch at the diner, Xavier drove them back to his cousins' house. As he parked the car, he glanced toward Kylie's car and saw that it had two flat tires. His gut started churning and he had the sensation of being watched. Pulling the house keys from his pocket, he then lobbed them to Lachlan. "Get her inside quick."

He got out of the truck and searched the area, but he couldn't see anyone. Lachlan and Will must have picked up on his anxiety, and when they got her out of the truck, they surrounded her. Will stood at her back and Lach in front of her. He waited until they had her in the house before heading to her car. When Xavier crouched down to examine her flat tires, he saw that they had been slashed. He skirted the small vehicle and cursed when he saw the other two tires were also ruined. Pulling his cell phone out of his pocket, he called the Sheriff and explained what he had found.

"Okay, I'll be there soon," Luke said.

Just as he disconnected the call, Will came out. He also glanced around before approaching him.

"Fuck!" Will walked around Kylie's car, looking at the tires. "Do you think he knows where she is?"

"That would be my guess."

"How the hell would he have found her?" Will asked.

Xavier frowned as he thought over that question, and then his bodyguard training kicked in. "Help me search the car."

He and Will went over every inch of the vehicle. He was lying on his back in the gravel and just as he was about to give up having not found anything, he caught sight of a small metal circle attached to the inside of the wheel rim. Xavier tried to pull the bug off the steel, but it was so small and his fingers were so big it was impossible. "Have you got your knife on you?"

"Yeah, here." Will passed him the blade hilt-first and Xavier pushed the tip beneath the small metal disk. It popped off and into his hand. He wriggled out from beneath her car and stood up, opening his palm and showing Will what he'd found.

"Fucking asshole." Will began to pace. "It had to have been him that tried to burn Kylie in the tent."

"We can't let her out of our sight." Xavier once more searched the yard and beyond. If someone had been there, they were long gone now.

"You know she's gonna demand to know what's going on."

"Yeah, I know, and we are going to tell her. She can't keep herself safe if she isn't aware of what's happening."

The sound of tires crunching on the gravel drive drew his attention and he looked up, ready to pounce. The tension seeped away when he saw it was the sheriff.

Luke got out of his car and approached them.

"Thanks for coming out so fast, Luke." Xavier shook his hand in greeting and then handed over the tracker. Luke bagged the small disk and then studied the car.

"I'll get Sheriff Damon Osborn out here to fingerprint the car. I don't expect to find anything, but you never know. How is Kylie?"

"Kylie's fine, thanks for asking."

Kylie hurried over to them and gasped when she saw her car. "That fucking asshole wrecked my tires."

Xavier grabbed her around the waist and hauled her up against his body. "You shouldn't be out here, baby. We don't even know if the guy is still around. For all we know, he could have you in the sights of a rifle."

She shivered and he hugged her tighter, offering her comfort.

"Kylie, where are you?" Lachlan yelled as he bolted from the house, sounding frantic.

"She's out here," Xavier answered.

Lachlan stormed across the yard until he was standing in front of their woman. "The next time you go haring off tell me where you're going first. You scared the crap out of me."

Luke's grunt drew their attention, but he was looking at Kylie. "If you were my woman, I would spank your ass until it was red."

"What?" Kylie yelled in outrage. "Don't you dare try to tell me you spank Felicity, because there is no way in hell she would let you do that to her."

A smile spread across Luke's face and he replied. "Darlin', my wife takes great delight in goading me, Tom, and Billy into doing just that. The right sort of spanking adds spice in the bedroom."

Xavier nearly laughed when Kylie's cheeks turned pink with embarrassment. He wondered if she was imagining what it would be like to be laid over his lap so he could spank her sexy little bottom. From the way her chest rose and fell and her nipples peaked, she liked the idea.

Luke walked away to call Damon. Xavier spun Kylie around and cupped her cheek. "We'll get to your spanking later, baby, but right now I would feel better if you went back inside."

"Okay." She ran her hand down his chest before moving toward the house.

Lachlan's voice drifted toward him on the breeze. "I can't wait to lay my hands on that sexy little ass. We already know you like to get your ass smacked, don't we, sugar."

"Shut up, Lach," Kylie snapped.

Lachlan just grabbed her hand and pulled her inside, laughing all the while.

Damon arrived with the fingerprint kit and to their frustration there were no fingerprints to be found other than Kylie's. The men could tell by the size of the prints they were hers. They were small and feminine, but just to be on the safe side Damon took Kylie's prints, too.

Luke and Damon headed toward the front door to take their leave, but Luke looked back at him over his shoulder. "I'll get my deputies to do a regular drive-by, but until this asshole makes his next move, we don't know who we're looking for, and that makes our job so much harder. Just stay vigilant."

Xavier closed the door after waving good-bye to the sheriffs and then went in search of Kylie. He found her sitting in the kitchen with Will and Lachlan, drinking coffee. She was frowning at her mug.

"What's wrong, Kylie?"

"I'm sick and tired of being scared." She looked up at him and then to each of his brothers. "I want this bastard caught so that I can get on with my life. I don't want to have to spend the rest of my life looking over my shoulder."

"I can understand that, baby, but we don't want anything to happen to you. You mean the world to us, Kylie. It would kill me if this asshole got to you." Xavier reached for her hand and then drew a deep breath and released it again. He wasn't sure that now was the right time, but she needed to know how much he cared for her. "I love you, Kylie, and I want to spend the rest of my life with you."

Will slid off his chair and onto the floor at Kylie's feet. "I love you, too, sweet thang. I need you in my life."

Lachlan clasped her free hand in his. "I love you, too, sugar, so much. We want you to move into our ranch house with us."

"I–I…I care about you three, too." She sighed. "I just…"

"You don't have to say anything, baby. We just wanted you to know how we feel about you." Xavier squeezed her hand. Will stood up and then sat back on his chair.

Kylie frowned at him, looking unhappy, but Xavier could see the love she had for them in her eyes. She just wasn't ready to tell them how she felt yet. He and his brothers would bide their time because Xavier knew once she realized how she felt there would be no stopping her. They'd already seen how passionate and loving she was, and if they were patient, they would reap the rewards when she was ready to declare her feelings.

Although she was timid sometimes, beneath that fear was a tigress just waiting to emerge and he was going to be by her side when she unleashed the real Kylie Mailing.

* * * *

It had been so easy to plant a tracker on the trucks. He'd followed them to the ranch but made sure to keep a long way back so he wouldn't draw attention to himself. Once again his patience and diligence had paid off. He was currently in his motel room, sipping a beer while staring at the TV, but the show on the screen couldn't hold his attention. He'd had to wait until they entered the diner for lunch before he could get close to the black truck. It would have been too risky to do it at the ranch with no other people around. He'd parked his rental car two blocks down and then walked along the street, looking around like a tourist.

When he'd been near the truck, he'd stumbled and gone down on his knees. While he was down, he had carefully applied superglue to the back of the tracker and then had placed his hand on the wheel rim and made it look like he was using the vehicle to gain his feet. Just as he stood, a deep voice had spoken from behind and it had taken all his effort not to have shown the anger he felt.

"Are you all right, sir? Are you hurt?"

He'd turned around to face one of the sheriffs. "I'm fine, thank you. Just took a little tumble is all."

"I haven't seen you around here before. Are you new in town?"

"No, sir, just passing through on my way to Denver to visit the folks. Your little town is very picturesque and I thought to take a look-see while stretching my legs."

"Where are you from?"

"Blanding, Utah."

"Well, you enjoy your walk and drive careful."

"Yes, sir, I will. You have a nice day now." He hurried back to his car and headed for the house, keeping an eye out for the hick sheriff. Again he'd parked his car out of sight and kept within the trees lining the road, in case someone came along, but no one had. He'd placed trackers on the other two trucks and then left a message for the bitch by slashing all four of her tires. Time was running out for her. He rubbed his hands together in anticipation.

Chapter Eleven

Kylie watched Xavier pace as he waited for his call. He had put in an offer through the estate agent to the owner of the ranch three days ago and was just waiting for confirmation. The agent had told him the vendor was keen to sell, since he had moved states to be closer to his son and daughter and their families. Kylie was excited on her men's behalf because they wanted that ranch so badly and couldn't wait to set up their own cattle breeding operation.

As she watched Xavier's restlessness, she finally admitted to herself that she was deeply in love with the Badon brothers and wanted to spend the rest of her life with them. Being with them had given her courage she'd never thought to see in herself. She no longer panicked when she was in a crowd and hadn't had a panic attack since the dinner at the Slick Rock hotel. And the more she thought about her situation with the fucker stalking her, the angrier she got. There was no way in hell she was going to live in fear for the rest of her life.

Just as she opened her mouth, Xavier's cell phone rang.

"Hello."

Kylie watched as a slow smile spread across Xavier's face and she knew his offer had been accepted. Will and Lachlan came rushing into the room but stayed quiet while Xavier spoke.

"Yes, ma'am, thank you so much. I'll be in this afternoon with a deposit check to sign all the paperwork. Two is perfect. Thank you, Ms. Jones, I'll see you then."

"We got the ranch house?" Will asked and Kylie was sure the question was rhetorical since the answer was already obvious, but she wasn't about to dampen his excitement.

"We got it," Xavier replied. He rushed over to her, scooped her off the lounge, and spun her around.

"Wow, I'm so happy for you all," Kylie said.

Will and Lach surrounded her when Xavier stopped spinning her, and she ended up sandwiched between three men, right where she wanted to be.

"Why don't we all go to the real estate office," Will suggested as he placed a kiss on the top of her head and stepped back. "We can pick up the keys and take Kylie to the house while you finalize the paperwork."

"That's a great idea," Xavier said. "I want you to start making a list of what we're going to need, baby. We have some furniture in storage, but we are going to need more."

"All my things are in storage, too," Kylie said. "Between the four of us we may have everything we need."

Lachlan gripped her shoulders, turned her around, and looked down into her eyes. "Are you saying what I think you're saying, sugar?"

"I don't know," Kylie teased and smiled at him. "Why don't you tell me what you're thinking?"

"Are you going to move in with us, Kylie?"

"Yes."

Lachlan picked her up until her feet left the floor and she wrapped her arms around his neck and her legs around his waist. "I love you, sweetheart. You've made me very happy."

Kylie placed her lips on his and kissed him. It didn't take long before he took over and devoured her mouth.

"Hey bro, let us have some of that sweet sugar, too." Will pulled her away from Lach and cradled her in his big muscular arms and then he kissed her.

Kylie sighed with arousal and contentment as he pulled away, and then Xavier was there. He lowered her feet back to the floor, bent her over his arm and ravaged her mouth. By the time he released her lips, her body was quivering with desire, and if it wasn't for the fact they had to get going, she would have asked them to make love with her.

"We'll get back to this later, baby, but we don't want to be late getting to the real estate agent's. You can ride with me in my truck and then go to the ranch with Will and Lach." Xavier slapped her ass as she hurried away to get her purse and decided she may just have to be bad to get more of the same.

* * * *

Will ushered Kylie through the front door to the ranch and watched as she did another exploration and began taking notes. Lachlan had headed upstairs to the bedrooms to take measurements and he wanted to go over the plumbing to make sure the pipes were sound. Kylie looked up at him as she finished making another note on her pad. "What is it you want to do?"

When he explained, she made a shooing motion with her hand. "You don't have to hover. I'll be fine here in the kitchen."

"I don't want to leave you alone, sweet thang."

"I'm safe here, Will. There is no one else around and you and Lach are only a yell away. Go on and do what you have to. With the three of us working, we'll get done a lot faster."

"Okay." Will kissed her on the cheek. "I'll lock the front door, but if you hear any little sound, you holler right away, all right?"

"Okay."

"Love you, honey." Will hurried upstairs. He and Lachlan had brought their tape measures as well as a pen and paper and spent the next half hour measuring the bathrooms and checking the plumbing. The pipes and fixtures were sound and he was pleased by the size of the master bath. The owner had updated the bathrooms a couple of years ago, and they only needed a fresh coat of paint. The shower was big enough for all four of them and there was also a large, square spa bath with steps leading up to it, and the vanity was inset with two sinks. He couldn't wait to get Kylie into that big tub.

Lachlan stepped into the bath just as Will finished inspecting the ceiling fan. "Where's Kylie?"

"In the kitchen."

"I was just down there." Lachlan frowned and then hurried out with Will following behind.

"Kylie," Will yelled, "where'd you get to, sugar?"

"Kylie, if you're playing with us, you'd better stop now. You're scaring me, sweet thang," Lachlan shouted.

* * * *

Kylie studied the sketch she made of the kitchen and then glanced around at reality. The whole thing needed to be gutted. It looked like something out of a seventies sitcom. The bench top was cracked orange Formica and the stove was so ancient she wondered if it still worked. As she walked over and pulled the oven open, she heard a noise behind her. She was about to turn toward it, but she didn't get the chance. A hand covered her mouth and something pierced the skin at the side of her neck and then her legs were giving out. Her vision blurred and it took great effort to turn her head and look up.

A big stranger stood over her and that was her last sight before she succumbed to the darkness.

* * * *

It had been so easy to sneak into the house through the back door. The lock had been child's play, and he'd had it open in seconds. He'd searched the bottom story and the stupid bitch hadn't even been aware of his presence. After making sure the two men with her weren't close by—he'd heard their footsteps on the floor above—he snuck into the kitchen. Her back was toward him and she was just pulling open the oven door when he stuck her with the sedative. He covered her mouth in case she cried out, but she just stared at him with shock and since the sedative he injected into her was fast working and he'd probably given her more than the required dosage for her height and weight, her legs buckled beneath her and she slumped to the floor. She looked up at him through glazed eyes and then her eyes closed.

He bent down, hefted her into his arms, and then slung her over his shoulder and rushed toward the back door. Her head connected with the wooden door frame as he hurried through the door, but he didn't slow down.

It took him nearly ten minutes to get to his car, which he'd parked on a gravel back road that didn't see much use. He'd studied the surrounding area on the Internet when he'd first seen the ranch so he wouldn't have to use the main road and draw attention to himself, and his homework had paid off. He pushed her into the backseat of the car and then got into the driver's seat.

Just as he turned onto the main road, a black truck passed him by. The driver looked at him but he didn't think the asshole had seen him. Besides why would anyone take note of a stranger just passing through?

He sighed with relief when he turned onto Highway 141 heading in a northeasterly direction, back toward Mountain Village and his motel room.

This was going to be so much fun.

* * * *

Xavier looked at the man driving the car toward Slick Rock. Something about him looked familiar, but he couldn't remember where he'd seen him before. He took note of the license plate and filed it away.

He couldn't wait to see Kylie in their new house again, even if it was only to see her making notes. She had entrenched herself in his heart and soul so fast and had finally conceded to move in with him and his brothers. The next step would be to ask her to marry them, but he was going to have to hold off on that for a while.

Just as he pulled to a stop in front of the house the door burst open, and Will and Lachlan ran toward him. "What's going on?" he asked as he got out.

"Kylie's missing," Will said in a hoarse voice.

"Fuck. Call Luke." He locked his knees so they wouldn't buckle. "Get him to run a plate." He rattled off the number when Will began to talk to the sheriff. Then Xavier turned to Lachlan. "Guns. Hurry."

Lachlan ran into the house, and by the time Will was off the phone with the sheriff, Lachlan was jogging from the house with a black duffle bag slung over his shoulder.

Xavier's stomach was roiling with fear and he felt sick to his stomach. Intuition kicked in and he got back into his truck. "Get in."

Lachlan jumped into the backseat and Will rushed around to the front. "Luke will call as soon as he has anything on that plate. Whose is it?"

"I don't know. I passed a guy going in the opposite direction when I was coming here," Xavier answered and pushed the pedal to the metal.

"What did he look like?" Lach asked.

"He was big, like you, Will, with black hair, and I'd guess around six three and two hundred and thirty pounds, and he had a mustache."

"You think he had Kylie?" Will asked.

Xavier nodded slowly. "I'd bet my truck on it. I only passed a few cars on my way here, and he was the only one I didn't recognize at all."

Will threw his hands in the air. "But how the hell did he find Kylie all the way out at the ranch?"

Lachlan chimed in from the backseat. "The same way he found out that Kylie was in Slick Rock. Pull over." When Xavier hesitated,

Lachlan's voice became more frantic. "There's a tracker on this truck, I know there is. Pull over."

Xavier slammed on the brakes and came to a screeching halt. All three of them got out of the car and searched every inch of the truck.

"I got it." Lachlan pried the bug from the wheel rim with his knife, placed the small device on the road and crushed it beneath the heel of his boot.

"Let's move."

Xavier sped through the town of Slick Rock, being careful of the people walking along the streets, and then picked up even more speed as he hit Highway 141. Just as he hit one hundred and twenty miles an hour, his cell phone rang.

Will hit the hands-free button and Sheriff Luke Sun-Walker's voice filled the cab. "The car is a rental and was leased in Sheridan in the name of Parker Smythe. It turns out that the rape victim is Smythe's stepson, Richard Harrow."

"Jesus. Any wonder the guy isn't talking? He's probably scared shitless. That asshole had probably threatened to kill him."

"Yeah," Luke sighed. "I'll get onto the police in Sheridan and make sure the victim and his mother are protected. The asshole used his credit card to book a room at the Mountain Village motel, nearly two hours from here. My deputies just finished running a check on him. This guy served in the army, so he's probably packing heat. Damon and I are on our way, and I've contacted the Mountain Village sheriff. Where are you?"

"In the truck on 141 heading toward Mountain Village."

"Don't you do anything until we get there, Xavier. The last thing I want to do is have to arrest your ass."

"What would you do if this asshole had Felicity?" Xavier asked angrily.

"Shit, just don't go getting your asses shot off." Luke disconnected the call.

* * * *

Kylie groaned as a drum beat in her skull. She was really thirsty and her mouth was so dry it felt like her tongue was cleaving to her palate. She shivered and tried to curl into a ball, but she couldn't move. It was hard work to open her eyes, and when she did, she wished she hadn't. She was tied to a bed in what looked to be a motel room, and there was a cloth shoved between her lips and tied around her head.

The man who had kidnapped her was sitting in a chair across the room, eating a hamburger and drinking a beer while he watched the television. The noise from the TV set must have muffled her groan, because he didn't look her way. In between bites of his burger it looked like he was talking, but she couldn't hear what he was saying. She wondered if he was talking to the TV or himself. He must have felt her watching him, because he turned his head and looked at her. When he smiled she could see the masticated food in his mouth and wanted to throw up. She turned her head away as her stomach roiled.

"You didn't think I'd find you, did you, bitch? I'm a lot smarter than you are. Did you think I was going to leave you alive so you could testify against me? You're just as worthless as every other female alive. The only thing a woman is good for is spreading her legs. I'm gonna have some fun with you before I kill you. I'm not letting you put me behind bars because of that little fucker.

"He'll never say anything against me. Do you wanna know why?" He laughed and the sound grated on her already shredded nerves. The guy was obviously out of his mind. "Because I'm his step daddy. He may be all grown up, but he still knows better than to rat me out. He knows I'll slit his throat before he can speak up."

Kylie had to concentrate on breathing through her nose so she wouldn't vomit. The thought of the young man being violated by someone in a position of trust was wholly evil. She turned back when he didn't speak again and found his eyes once more glued to the idiot box. Taking advantage of his inattention, she straightened her fingers, tucked her thumb against her palm and pulled. The rope around her wrists bit into her flesh but she kept right on pulling. Blood seeped from her torn flesh, but she didn't care. She ignored the pain and hoped the fluid would help lubricate the hemp and she would be able to get her hands free. Just as she got the rope around the thickest part of her hand, he moved.

He moved fast for such a big man. Because one moment he was across the room staring at the TV and the next he was on the bed straddling her hips with a knife against her chest.

"You didn't think I was paying attention, did you, slut?" He chuckled but there was no humor in the sound, only madness. He slid the tip of the knife between the buttons of her shirt and cut them off one by one. When they were gone, he pushed the material aside.

"You've got nice tits on you, bitch. I'll bet those men fucking you would hate to see them marred."

Kylie was shaking with fear and she panted for breath. But since she had a cloth shoved into her mouth and could only breathe through her nose, she was feeling light-headed. The fear threatened to take over, but then she remembered how it felt to be held and cherished by men who loved her. She had only just found them and she wasn't about to let her panic take over until she couldn't think straight. She remembered being surrounded by her three men when they had found out the ranch house was theirs and then she began to get angry. There was no way she was giving up without a fight. If this asshole was going to kill her, then she was going down kicking and screaming.

He sliced the front of her bra in half and slid the knife over her skin. She watched and waited for her chance. It didn't take long, because he was so intent on staring at her breasts and not at her eyes.

As he lowered his head to her chest, Kylie reared up and slammed her forehead into his nose. He howled with rage and she felt satisfaction when she saw the blood pouring out of his nostrils and his nose askew. She'd broken the asshole's nose.

She watched as he raised the knife, as if in slow motion, and then began to arc it down. At the last second she twisted around, wrenching her shoulder and further tearing the skin on her wrist, and then she cried out as agony assailed her. He'd stabbed her, but she'd moved fast enough so that the knife glanced off her shoulder blade, flew out of his grasp, and landed on the bed, only feet from her. She used every ounce of strength and energy she could, bucking and twisting, trying to get him to fall off of her. His fist smashed into her face and then his hand was squeezing around her throat and her vision began to waver. Then he leisurely grabbed the knife from beside her, the metal of the blade glinted under the light, and she waited for more excruciating pain.

* * * *

Will's hands were trembling and he felt guilty as hell that Kylie had been kidnapped under his watch. If he hadn't left her alone in the kitchen while he'd gone to inspect the plumbing, she would be safe. He would never forgive himself if something happened to her because of him. There was a huge knot of anxiety in his chest and he didn't think he'd ever breathe normally again.

He unlocked the glove compartment of Xavier's truck and pushed the hidden button in the back. A hidden compartment popped open. Lachlan unzipped the duffel and pulled out three nine millimeter Glocks and six clips of ammo. He passed two guns and four clips to Will before loading his own weapon and stashing the extra clip in his pocket. They were only minutes away from the Mountain Village Motel and he wanted to be prepared.

Xavier didn't pull into the motel parking lot. Instead he parked a hundred yards down the street. Will handed Xavier the loaded Glock and extra clip, and they got out of the truck. None of them spoke as they ran toward the motel. Luke must have called the local sheriff because he was standing on the street waiting for them.

"Are you Xavier, Lachlan, and Will Badon?"

"We are," Lach replied.

"I'm Sheriff Cal Shone. Parker has her tied to the bed in room five. It looks like your woman is unconscious and the perp was eating a burger and watching TV. My deputy is keeping watch. I want you three to stay back. I don't want any of you getting hurt."

"Has he got a weapon?" Will asked.

"I don't know, son."

"Are you married, Sheriff?" Xavier asked the middle-aged man.

"Yes, sir, going on twenty years now."

"Would you stand back and watch someone else rescue your wife?"

"Now look here…"

"Sheriff, we are professionally trained bodyguards," Lachlan said. "We are packing registered weapons and we know how to use them."

The sheriff looked to each of them and smiled. "Well, come on then."

They followed the sheriff into the parking lot, where he stopped and pointed out room five. Lachlan and Will took up position beside the door, glad that the drapes covered most of the window, and Xavier stood in front of the entrance, ready to kick it in. Just as he raised his foot, a loud bellow of pain and fury rent the air.

Xavier kicked the door in and rushed forward, and Will and Lachlan hurried in after him. Rage like he'd never felt before coursed through him as he heard a muffled feminine scream and saw the asshole with his hand around Kylie's throat, choking her. The fucker raised his arm again, ready to plunge the knife into their woman.

Xavier ran forward, grabbed the hand holding the knife, and tried to wrestle it away. Will had his gun raised, ready to shoot, but with Xavier in the way, he couldn't risk hitting his brother. Xavier managed to get the knife and flung it across the room. Parker removed his hand from around Kylie's throat and reached to the middle of his back. He came up with a .38 and pointed it at Kylie's head.

"Back off now or I'll pull the trigger."

Xavier released his hand and placed his palm up in front in surrender then stepped back. Lachlan moved toward the bed, drawing the fucker's attention and also the aim of his gun. That was just what Will been waiting for. He aimed and fired and watched dispassionately as a hole formed in the middle of Parker's forehead before he slumped down on top of Kylie and the bed.

"Call the paramedics," Xavier yelled to the sheriff.

Will secured his gun and rushed toward their woman. Lachlan pulled Parker off of Kylie and removed the gag from her mouth, and between the three of them, removed the rope from around her wrists and ankles. Kylie didn't look like she was breathing and her lips were tinged blue. Will pressed his ear to her chest and then tipped her head back, squeezed her nostrils and opened her mouth. He forced air into her lungs three times and then turned his head to watch her chest. He repeated the action three more times and then sagged in relief when she coughed and began to breathe on her own.

The paramedics pushed into the room and began to assess Kylie. They covered the stab wound on her back, placed an oxygen mask over her face, and when they had her hooked up to an IV, they lifted her to the gurney and wheeled her out.

"Where are you taking her?" Xavier asked in a raspy voice.

"Telluride Medical Center."

"Will, go with her. One of us needs to be with her when she wakes up."

Will followed the paramedics to the ambulance, climbed in, and sat near her head. He held her hand for the full seven-minute trip and didn't want to let go when they arrived but held back as they wheeled her away.

He was going to have nightmares for the rest of his life after finding the woman he loved on the verge of death.

Chapter Twelve

Kylie spent a total of three days in the hospital and none of her men left her side. Friends she didn't realize she had made the long drive to visit and gave her get-well gifts. Luke Sun-Walker arrived to take her statement and then lectured her men about rushing in where angels feared to tread. But Kylie was glad her men had the skills to protect her and had been able to rescue her.

If she was ever in a situation like that again—God forbid—she would not hesitate to trust them to take care of her. The doctor had just left after giving her a final examination and the nurse was already processing her release forms, which had been signed.

Her throat and neck were sore, but there wasn't any permanent damage. She had stitches in her shoulder blade, but she had been lucky that no tendons had been impaired, and since she was healthy, her bones were strong and hadn't suffered any chips or fractures. She was good to go.

Kylie pushed the covers aside and moved her legs to hang over the side of the bed. Will rushed over to help her and she let him. He'd already told her he felt guilty for leaving her alone in the ranch house and she had told him what had happened wasn't his fault, but she wasn't sure if she had gotten through to him.

Xavier told her how she hadn't been breathing and Will had performed the kiss of life. If it hadn't been for her men rescuing her and Will breathing for her, she would be dead. As far as she was concerned, they were her heroes, her knights in shining armor. Now, if she could only get them to believe her.

"Are you okay, sweet thang?" Will asked as he helped her dress. She'd had a shower earlier that morning and had been waiting impatiently to be released from the hospital.

"I'm fine, Will. Where are Xavier and Lach?"

"Xavier's gone to bring the truck around to the front and Lach is finishing up the paperwork."

"I'm here, sugar. Xavier has the truck out front. Are you ready?"

"You have no idea." Kylie smiled. "Quick, let's get out of here before they change their minds."

Kylie thanked the hospital staff for taking such good care of her. They smiled, but when she left she noticed it wasn't her the nurses had their eyes on, but her men. She couldn't blame them. Her men were hot.

Will lifted her up into the backseat of the truck and got in behind her. He patted his knee and looked at her. "Why don't you put your head on my lap and take a nap, sweetheart? It'll take nearly two hours before we get back home."

"You're kidding, right? I've had more sleep in the last three days than I've had in the last three weeks."

"Then come over here and cuddle with me, honey."

Kylie moved to the middle of the seat and snuggled with Will. That was the last thing she remembered until she woke up in her bedroom in Eva's house.

Another four days passed before Kylie was able to get the stitches out of her back. Her men had been in and out of the house often, but one of them was with her at all times. She had asked them what they were up to and they had just smiled and replied, "It's a surprise."

She was starting to get antsy and wanted to know what was going on, but none of them would tell her. Lachlan drove her to the doctor's and after her sutures were removed, he drove the opposite direction from Eva's house.

"Are we going to the ranch?"

"We are."

"Good, I can't wait until we can move in. We have so much to do. When can we get someone in to look at the kitchen?"

"Soon, Kylie."

When he pulled up near the porch steps Xavier and Will were standing on the veranda, waiting for them. Will came down the steps, opened her door and lifted her out. He hugged her tight and then handed her off to Xavier. Xavier held her against his big, warm, muscular body and then with an arm around her waist led her up the steps.

"Are the stitches out, baby? Did the doctor give you the all clear?"

"Yeah, I'm all healed."

"Why don't we go inside?" Lachlan suggested and held the front door open for her.

Kylie entered the entrance hall and froze when she saw the furniture in the living room.

"Oh. Wow, this looks awesome. Did you get your things out of storage?" She turned to face her men and then registered what she had seen and spun back around again. "You know, I have a lounge suite exactly the same as this one."

Kylie moved across and sat down on the leather cherrywood-colored lounge. When she sat it felt like her own lounge. She ran her hand over the arm and felt the little notch where a tear in the leather had been repaired. She leaned in close to study where it had been melded together again.

The silence drew her gaze and she lifted her head to see all three of her men watching her. And the penny finally dropped.

"Oh. My. God," Kylie squealed and ran over to her lovers, gathering them close. "This is my lounge suite, isn't it?"

"Yeah, baby, it is."

"How did you arrange this? How did you know where my things were being stored?"

Will looked at her sheepishly. “I had Felicity go through your purse while you were in the hospital, and with help from her husbands they arranged for your things to be brought here.”

“Thank you.” Kylie reached up and kissed Xavier’s cheek and then turned to Lachlan. She grabbed his shirt and yanked him down so she could reach him and kissed his chin. “Thank you.” She let his shirt go and threw herself at Will, knowing he would catch her and he did. She wrapped her arms around his neck and kissed his lips. “Thank you all so much.”

Will lowered her feet back to the floor. “You’re welcome, sweet thang.”

Kylie glanced about and saw that a fresh coat of paint adorned the walls. She looked back over to them and smiled before racing into the kitchen and skidding to a halt on the polished hardwood floors. A gasp of awe escaped as she took in the wonder of what she was seeing. The seventies kitchen was no more. In its place were brand-new oak cupboards and state-of-the-art stainless-steel appliances and a dark granite bench top, exactly like she had drawn on her note pad. Tears of admiration streamed down her face as love and joy filled her heart.

The three Badon brothers had told her they loved her and though she knew they cared for her, she had been a little skeptical about whether it was actually love. Seeing how they went out of their way to please her and how they had come after her when Parker had abducted and tried to kill her, left no doubt in her mind how much she really meant to them. She had decided while recuperating in the hospital to stop being scared, to grab hold of the best things that had ever happened to her and not let go, but she hadn’t found the right moment to let them know how she felt about them. *Until now.*

Kylie turned to find them standing just inside the doorway watching her, and she took a deep, steadying breath as she wiped the moisture from her cheeks. “Will, you are such a deeply caring man and I know you still blame yourself for leaving me alone that day, but if you hadn't you would probably be dead. He would have killed you and there would have been a huge hole in my heart for the rest of my life. You saved my life, baby. You breathed life back into me. I love you with my heart and soul."

"I love you, too, sweet thang," Will replied, and she could see the moisture in his eyes.

"Lachlan, you are so serious most of the time, but then you will come out with something to make me laugh and you are always trying to lighten my load. You mean everything to me. I love you, Lach."

"I love you, too, sugar."

She looked up into Xavier's blue eyes. "Xavier you can be a pain in the ass with your arrogance and how you try to tell me what to do, but I know that you care about me and only want to keep me safe. I love you just the way you are and wouldn't change anything about you." She looked at all her men. "I wouldn't change a thing about any of you. I love you all just the way you are."

Xavier stepped forward and took one of her hands into his. "I love you, Kylie Mailing. I didn't realize how empty my life was until the night you bumped into me and nearly fell on your ass. You started spitting bile at me from the first night and grabbed me by the balls, and my heart followed quickly behind."

Xavier looked at Will and then Lachlan and nodded. As one they all kneeled down in front of her. Will took her hand from Xavier's and Lachlan held her free hand. Xavier dipped into his jeans pocket and then held up a small open jeweler's box.

"Kylie, we've been waiting for you for so long and now that you are finally in our lives, we want to spend whatever time we have left on this earth with you by our sides. We love you, Kylie Mailing. Will you please do us the very great honor of becoming our wife?" Xavier asked.

"Yes." Kylie was only able to whisper her answer as emotion clogged her throat. "I would love to marry you all and spend the rest of my life with you all by my side."

Will removed the emerald and diamond ring from the box and placed it on her left ring finger and then he pulled her into his arms and kissed her.

Kylie lost herself in Will as his tongue thrust into her mouth and danced with hers. She felt him lifting her but didn't stop kissing him as he carried her to wherever he wanted. When he slowed the kiss and lifted his head, they were both breathing heavily and she looked around for her other loves. How they had moved so fast she had no clue, but they were in the master bedroom, which had the biggest wooden framed bed she had ever seen and Xavier and Lachlan were lying on the covers, totally naked.

"Yes," Kylie said as she stared at her fiancés' gloriously nude bodies.

"Yes what, baby?" Xavier asked.

"Make love to me."

"With pleasure, sugar," Lachlan held out his hand and she walked toward him and placed hers in his.

Will came up behind her and began to undress her. He undid the button and zipper on her jeans while Lachlan released the buttons on her shirt with his free hand. When she was totally naked, Will lifted her onto the bed into the middle of the mattress and then moved around and got up on the end.

"We want to make love with you at the same time, honey. Will you trust us not to hurt you?" Lach asked.

"I trust you all with my life," she replied without hesitation.

Xavier gently pushed on her shoulder until she was lying flat on her back and then he started kissing her. Will rubbed his hands up and down her thighs, nudging them apart, and Lach latched on to her nipples, one with his mouth and the other he squeezed between finger and thumb.

Kylie went up in flames. The more they touched and kissed her the more she burned. She moaned into Xavier's mouth when Will licked her pussy and laved her clit, and she cried out when Lach pinched one nipple and scraped his teeth over the other.

Xavier released her mouth and began to lick and nibble down her neck and then her men withdrew all at the same time. Will helped her to turn over and then guided her until she was on her hands and knees. He swapped places with Lachlan and began to play with a breast and kiss her mouth. Xavier ran a hand over her back and played with her other nipple while Lachlan massaged her ass cheeks.

"A little cold, sugar."

Kylie groaned when Lachlan's cold, wet fingers stroked over her anus and then she moaned as he began to penetrate her. She felt so connected with her men as they touched, kissed, stroked, and loved her. By the time Lachlan had stretched her ass out, she was frantic with need. Xavier moved over to the edge of the bed and Lachlan picked her up while Will moved into position and then Lachlan helped to lower her over Will's hard condom-covered cock.

"Oh yes," Kylie moaned. "You stretch me to the point of pain, but you feel so good inside me."

"You feel like heaven, sweet thang." Will panted and then groaned as Kylie lowered over him all the way. "Come here, Kylie." Will tilted her head and kissed her hungrily and she realized he was trying to distract her so she wouldn't tense up.

Lach's condom-covered cock pushed at her back entrance and then her ass began to burn.

"Look at me, baby," Xavier demanded and she lifted her mouth from Will's to meet his gaze. He was kneeling back on his heels on the bed and nearly in the right position for her to suck his cock. She licked her lip in anticipation. "You can have my cock in a minute, but I need to watch you while Lach takes your ass."

Lach pushed in slowly, stopping regularly to give her time to adjust to the foreign intrusion, and she kept her eyes on Xavier's. By the time he had his cock all the way in, Kylie was on the verge of climax.

"Oh, I'm so full. I need more. I love you all so much. Please, move," she sobbed, finding it hard to string words together but frantic for them to relieve the ache building inside.

Xavier gripped the base of his cock and fisted a handful of her hair close to her scalp. "Suck my cock, baby."

She opened her mouth and took him in as far as she could.

"Fucking amazing," he growled as her mouth slid back up his shaft and she swirled her tongue around the head.

"You should feel her ass," Lachlan panted as he withdrew. Will shoved his cock forward into her pussy and as he withdrew Lach slid back into her rectum.

The three men set up a rhythm of advance and retreat, one shoving into her pussy while the other counterthrust into her ass and Xavier set a rhythm all of his own. The tension built at a rapid pace and there was nothing she could do to stop the approaching bliss. She let go of the tight control she'd kept on herself, putting herself into the safe keeping of the men she loved.

"I'm coming, baby, swallow my juices." Xavier gasped and then he roared and his semen exploded from the tip of his cock, and she drank down his salty essence. "Jesus, baby, you've wrecked me."

Kylie was only vaguely aware of Xavier flopping down beside her because her own release was upon her. She drew in a breath, tilted her head back, and screamed.

"Fuck yeah, sugar, milk the cum from my cock," Lachlan panted, and then he yelled as he filled the condom with his release.

"I love you, Kylie," Will shouted and then he, too, reached orgasm.

Kylie slumped down onto Will and closed her eyes with satiation.

She was right where she wanted to be, her heart captured by the loves of her life as they surrounded her in their safe and loving embrace.

THE END

WWW.BECCAVAN-EROTICROMANCE.COM

ABOUT THE AUTHOR

My name is Becca Van. I live in Australia with my wonderful hubby of many years, as well as my two children.

I read my first romance, which I found in the school library, at the age of thirteen and haven't stopped reading them since. It is so wonderful to know that love is still alive and strong when there seems to be so much conflict in the world.

I dreamed of writing my own book one day but, unfortunately, didn't follow my dream for many years. But once I started I knew writing was what I wanted to continue doing.

I love to escape from the world and curl up with a good romance, to see how the characters unfold and conflict is dealt with. I have read many books and love all facets of the romance genre, from historical to erotic romance. I am a sucker for a happy ending.

For all titles by Becca Van, please visit
www.bookstrand.com/becca-van

Siren Publishing, Inc.
www.SirenPublishing.com